"For what it's worth, I think you're pretty special, Rachel."

He could see her defenses spring up. "You shouldn't say that."

"Of course I should. It's true."

"We agreed to keep things profes

"I'm really starting to hate th
rein in his frustration. "I
won't make it disap

Her blue gaze turn

Around them, the ho   quiet.
Reaching out, he took   ands in his. "So
you're just going to pre   you don't feel anything
when my fingers touch yours." He linked their
fingers and pressed their palms together.

"That's right." But she swallowed hard.

"And it wouldn't make any difference if I stroked
your hair." He let go of her left hand and skimmed
his fingers lightly over the smooth strands above
her ear.

"No." Her fingers twitched in his grasp.

"So a simple kiss wouldn't matter at all."

She drew a deep breath. "Of course not."

"Okay, then." He leaned forward and set his lips
against hers...

Dear Reader,

While my husband served in the Navy, we lived in six different cities, and we moved to yet another location when he retired. Each move posed challenges—learning where to shop and how to get to school, finding piano teachers and the best place for pizza. Most important, we would be seeking new friends and discovering how our family could fit into the local community. You never really feel at home until you've established your special crowd, your "tribe."

The Marshall brothers have lived in Bisons Creek, Wyoming, all their lives. So when Dr. Rachel Vale comes to town to set up a medical clinic, Garrett Marshall makes it his mission to help her feel comfortable in her new setting. Local opinion holds that the doctor and the minister are a perfect match, and Garrett is inclined to agree. But Rachel isn't so easily persuaded, and past experience has left her wary of romantic complications. As a medical emergency at the Circle M Ranch brings them together, Garrett must find a way to convince this cautious woman that he can be trusted—with the safety of her patients and with her heart.

Mail from readers is always a delight. Feel free to contact me at my website, lynnettekentbooks.com, or at PO Box 204, Vass, North Carolina 28394.

Lynnette Kent

A MARRIAGE IN WYOMING

LYNNETTE KENT

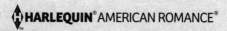

Recycling programs
for this product may
not exist in your area.

ISBN-13: 978-0-373-75620-9

A Marriage in Wyoming

Copyright © 2016 by Cheryl B. Bacon

This edition published by arrangement with Harlequin Books S.A.

For questions and comments about the quality of this book, please contact us at CustomerService@Harlequin.com.

Printed in U.S.A.

A child of the North Carolina mountains, **Lynnette Kent** seems destined to find herself living anywhere *but* the mountains. Her family moved to Florida when she was nine, inspiring her with a lifelong love of the ocean and a long day spent at the beach. After marrying a graduate of the US Naval Academy, she moved with him to Tennessee while he attended medical school and from there to Virginia, California and Washington, DC.

Now settled in southeastern North Carolina, Lynnette tries to remember that mountain flowers don't grow well in the heat of a Sandhills summer, that fall isn't an abrupt change of season but a gentle, lingering evolution, and that winter without snow can be...well, endured. With her two daughters married and on their own, she practices her nurturing skills with the six horses and five dogs on her farm. When she's not immersed in writing a book, or reading one, she mows grass, moves hay and fights a never-ending battle with weeds.

Books by Lynnette Kent

Harlequin American Romance

Christmas at Blue Moon Ranch
Smoky Mountain Reunion
Smoky Mountain Home
A Holiday to Remember
Jesse: Merry Christmas, Cowboy
A Convenient Proposal

The Marshall Brothers

A Wife in Wyoming
A Husband in Wyoming

Chapter One

Funny how a day could change so quickly.

One moment Garrett Marshall was enjoying a beautiful Monday morning in July. He was putting the finishing touch on the converted building that would now house the new medical clinic for the little town of Bisons Creek—a hand-carved and painted sign created by his artist brother, Dylan, announcing the medical practice of Dr. Rachel Vale. Garrett measured the sign and the space, calculating exactly where the hangers should go. Then he took his hammer and the first nail, cocked his wrist...

And slammed the face of the hammer directly onto his thumb.

"Damnation!" The hammer clanked to the floor of the porch as Garrett swore. Sucking on the injured finger, he glanced around to see if anybody had heard him. According to his congregation, ministers didn't use such words, except in their sermons about the rewards of sin. Garrett didn't want to shatter their illusions if he could help it.

Luckily, no one had been within earshot, but as he bent to pick up the hammer, a dusty green SUV pulled up to the curb in front of the clinic and stopped. The driver came around the hood of the vehicle to survey the building. "There's no sign," she called. "How will people find the place?"

"I'm working on it," Garrett called back. "Give me two minutes." Aware that he was being watched, he picked up the hammer he'd dropped and blew out a breath. "Focus…"

He didn't hit his thumb again, though it took a few extra taps to get the first hanger firmly seated. The second went in with a little more finesse. Then he picked up the sign and hung it on the wall. "There you go."

When he turned, he found the woman standing on the porch with him—and the close-up view took his breath away. Bright blue eyes and rosy lips, long hair in a shade of red he labeled russet, creamy skin and a curvy figure accentuated by a T-shirt and shorts…it all added up to perfection, as far as Garrett was concerned.

"It's a nice sign," she said, "but I'm not sure it will be visible from the street."

She was also, he gathered, rather picky. "There will be a bigger, freestanding sign in the yard for the Bisons Creek Medical Clinic. It's not quite finished."

"That sounds great." Smiling, she extended a hand. "I'm Rachel Vale."

"Garrett Marshall." Taking off his hat, he held her right hand in his and squeezed, but then couldn't prevent a wince.

Her warm smile became a worried frown. "What's wrong?"

"I hammered my thumb just before you arrived. Don't worry—"

"Your right thumb?" She brought his hand closer to her face. "Are you left-handed?"

"I am, as a matter of fact." He was also flushing in embarrassment at this point.

Dr. Vale hadn't noticed, her attention being concentrated on his thumb. Her fingers were cool and gentle on his skin, and very clean. As she bent her head, he caught the crisp herbal scent of her shampoo. Unobtrusively, he drew in a deeper breath. *Very nice.*

"Has the pain diminished since it happened?"

"Yes, definitely diminished. I'm fine, really. Just feeling stupid." *Nothing like looking clumsy in front of a gorgeous professional woman.* He might be a pastor, but he had his pride.

"It'll be bruised." She released his hand. "Ice would be a good idea. I'd offer some, but I have no idea if I even have any ice."

"I'm okay," Garrett assured her. Her touch seemed to linger on his skin. "Shall I let you inside? Or do you have the keys?"

"The mayor sent me a set," she said, pulling a key ring out of her back pocket. "Let's see how this works." With a couple of quick twists of her wrist, the door swung open. "Ta-da! My own clinic." She nodded toward the interior. "Want to share my first tour?"

For another smile, he'd hang around all day. "My pleasure." He followed her into the waiting room, where a pass-through window opened into the receptionist's office. "This building used to be a general store," he said as she surveyed the space. "It had been empty for years but wasn't too hard to clean up and renovate into what you needed. Mostly a matter of putting up walls and doors, dropping the ceiling and laying new vinyl over the concrete."

"That all sounds pretty labor-intensive to me. I like the light gray walls and charcoal floor. Very soothing." She went through the door patients would use into the back hallway, where there were two examining rooms, a laboratory and an office. "You've made a big effort."

"We're pretty excited to have a medical clinic. Driving to Kaycee or Casper isn't an easy option for some folks."

The doctor nodded as she peeked behind cabinet doors, opened drawers and examined the boxes of equipment stacked on the counter. "I grew up in a small town, with no local doctor and a mother who had health issues. Getting to and from her appointments could take up most of a day. And as a doctor, I've experienced firsthand how beneficial it is for patients in an isolated community to have accessible health care. Problems can be handled relatively easily in the office rather than exacerbated by patients' reluctance to make a long drive, especially the elderly. It's one of the issues I specifically want to address in my career."

Talk about commitment! Garrett thought she might be too good to be true. "I'm glad to hear that. We have our share of older folks in Bisons Creek." He followed her down the hallway. "I understand your training is in family medicine?"

"At the University of Washington, in Seattle. I've also worked in small towns in Idaho and Montana." She stood at the door to the office. "But never with an office this nice. There's even a desk and an armchair and carpet, as if this were a real doctor's study. Next I'll be thinking I'm a real doctor."

"That's what we're hoping anyway."

"I do have certificates," she said, grinning at him. "I can fake it pretty well."

"I won't tell." He returned the grin with one of his own. Her bright blue gaze held his and there was a second when he could have sworn he felt the click of a connection between them.

Then she looked away and gestured at a cluster of boxes on the floor. "I'm glad my professional books arrived. I didn't have room for everything in the car. I'll have to buy some bookcases to put them on."

"Having carried them in here, I can say you'd better get heavy-duty shelves. Each of those boxes weighs a ton."

"And they cost a fortune to mail. I hope I don't have to ship them again for a long, long time."

"I like the sound of that. You're welcome for as long as you want to stay."

"Thanks." She crossed the hall to the lab area. The equipment she'd ordered was already in place. "Functional and efficient—just what I asked for. And there's a room set aside for the X-ray machine, right? I'm hoping that will be my first big purchase."

"Right here." Garrett opened the door to show her the windowless space. "We built it to the dimensions you gave us."

Eyes shining, she spread her arms wide. "Everything I could ask for. You've done a terrific job."

He held up a hand in protest. "I can't take too much credit. The whole town worked together on raising funds to restore the building."

"But you must be the town carpenter, right?"

"Um, no. Kimble Construction did most of the real work. I'm the minister at Bisons Creek Church. My brother built the sign and I said I'd hang it."

"Oh." Her glow of excitement seemed to dim. "Well... thank you for all your help." She walked away, toward the front of the clinic. "I'll let you get on with your day. I'm sure you have things to do."

Following, Garrett felt dismissed. "We do have a friend in common, though. Caroline Donnelly, who recommended you for the job, is my brother Ford's fiancée."

In the waiting room, she faced him again. "You're one

of the Marshall brothers. Now I see." She thawed slightly. "Caroline has talked a lot about all of you in her emails this summer. I understand you have a camp on your ranch for some of her at-risk kids."

"We do. And I should be getting back to them right now. I just wanted to be sure you had a sign to welcome you to town."

"I appreciate the effort. Really." But her pretty face was empty of expression. The contagious enthusiasm of a few minutes before had vanished. She held the door open and actually waved him out. "Have a good one."

"You, too." Garrett found himself on the porch, the door firmly shut behind him. Staring at the panel, he couldn't figure out what the heck had happened, why Rachel Vale's attitude had changed so fast—from friendly and outgoing to almost hostile. He didn't remember anything he'd said or done that accounted for the difference.

In fact, he'd been anticipating getting to know her better, maybe building up to the suggestion of a cup of coffee at the diner, or even some lunch. He'd been reflecting what a welcome addition to the Bisons Creek social scene she would be...

Funny how the tone of the day could change so fast.

After replacing his hammer and the package of nails in his toolbox, Garrett climbed behind the wheel of his truck, intending to head toward the Circle M Ranch, where he and his brothers lived and worked. But just as he put his hand on the key to start the engine, he heard a door slam. He glanced at the clinic to find Rachel Vale hurrying down the walk. She opened the back of her SUV and pulled out a large duffel bag, then came up to his truck.

She opened the rear passenger door. "I just got a call from Caroline. There's some kind of emergency at your place." After slinging the duffel into the backseat, she climbed in the front. "We need to get out there right away."

"Welcome to Bisons Creek," Garrett said, pulling out into street. "I can't tell you how glad I am that you're here."

"DID CAROLINE SAY what happened?" Garrett Marshall asked.

"Only that one of the kids was very sick," Rachel told him. "I didn't get any other details."

After a short, mostly silent drive out of town, they turned in underneath the iron arch of the Circle M Ranch. Though her mind was preoccupied with the situation waiting for her, Rachel could appreciate the landscape of rolling, grassy plains and the big blue sky stretching overhead.

"A beautiful setting," she said. "You must be proud of your property."

"Not so much proud as grateful." He smiled as he glanced over. "We feel pretty lucky to be able to take care of this parcel of land."

Even though he'd said he was a minister, he certainly looked the part of the traditional rancher—close-fitting jeans, a dark blue work shirt and the quintessential white Western hat. With medium brown hair in a conservative cut and those sharp blue eyes, he made a very attractive cowboy, for those who found the type appealing.

Telling herself she wasn't one of them, Rachel turned her gaze back to the view outside. "Has your family lived on the Circle M for generations?"

"No, as a matter of fact. My brothers and I lost both our parents before I was twelve. My oldest brother, Wyatt, was hired on here by Henry MacPherson, the man who owned the Circle M at that time. Eventually Henry had us all move out from town to live with him. When he died, he left the ranch to us. The Marshall brothers are relatively new to the ranching business, all told."

She saw buildings in the distance—a timber-sided house and a big red barn on the hill above it. "Mr. MacPherson must have thought very highly of you."

"Well, Wyatt is a responsible and dedicated worker— Henry knew he'd do his best for the place. The rest of us help out as much as we can, given our other responsibilities. Especially this summer, because Wyatt got bucked off a horse and broke a couple of bones in his back, so he's out of commission for the time being."

"That's too bad. I hope he's taking good care of himself."

They approached the sprawling, single-story house, where a group of teenagers had gathered on the porch, most of them staring at their phones. Garrett stopped the truck in front of the steps. Before he'd even shifted into park, Rachel swung out of her seat, pulled the duffel from the rear seat, then crossed to the door and knocked.

Dark-haired Caroline Donnelly opened the screen door. "Oh, Rachel, I'm so glad you're here. And so glad I could call you." Behind her was a blond man who looked enough like Garrett that he had to be one of his brothers. Handsome evidently ran in the Marshall family.

Rachel gave her friend a one-armed hug. "Me, too. What's going on?"

Across the room, a young girl lay bonelessly on the sofa.

"We were doing rodeo practice on the bucking barrel. Lena said she wanted to ride and walked over…but then she just sort of staggered and fell down. We carried her in and called an ambulance. And you."

"Smart thinking." Rachel knelt by the sofa. One deep breath of the fruity aroma surrounding the patient gave her all the information she needed. "Did she say anything?" From the front pocket of the duffel, she pulled out a glucometer to test Lena's blood glucose level.

"She was acting kinda crazy this morning." A tanned, black-haired boy sat in a recliner nearby. "I said she shouldn't ride, but she wouldn't listen." His dark eyes were wide with fear. "Is she okay?"

Caroline came over and put a hand on his shoulder. "We've got help now, Justino. Dr. Vale will know what to do."

"Did she eat breakfast?" Rachel asked. The blood-sugar result was high. And her blood pressure was low.

Justino shook his head. "She's been sick for a couple of days. Throwing up and stuff."

"Why didn't she say something?" Garrett asked. "Why didn't you?"

Rachel cut in. "She's quite slender. Has she always been thin?"

"Yeah. But she said her jeans are getting loose, even though she's been hungry a lot."

"And thirsty?" Rachel asked.

"Oh, yeah. She drinks all the time."

Lena fluttered her eyelashes and moved her head slightly.

"There you are," Rachel said. "Hi, Lena, I'm Dr. Vale. How are you?"

"So thirsty," Lena whispered without opening her eyes. "So tired."

Turning again to her bag, Rachel began pulling out materials—an IV bag of saline and tubing, a syringe and a bottle of insulin. "Raise her legs," she ordered over her shoulder. "Above her heart."

While the others bustled around to help her, she handed the IV bag to Justino. "Hold this up high." After inserting the needle into Lena's arm, Rachel attached the tubing and adjusted the flow. Then she drew up ten units of insulin and injected it into the IV. "You'll start to feel better soon," she told the girl. Lena didn't answer.

"That's all I can do," she said, getting to her feet. "She's got to get to the hospital. How long ago did you call the ambulance?"

"They should be here any minute," Caroline said. "What's wrong? Why did she collapse?"

"She's dehydrated and her blood glucose is very high. With fluids and insulin, though, she'll start to improve."

"Thank God," Garrett said. "And thank you." He glanced around the room. "These are my brothers, by the way. Ford's the blond in the green shirt and Wyatt's the one wearing the back brace."

Nods were exchanged and hands shaken, but Rachel quickly returned her attention to Lena, noting that her breathing had slowed and her blood pressure had come up slightly. Positive signs.

Finally, she heard the siren they'd been waiting for. "The ambulance is here, Lena. You'll be in the hospital in just a few more minutes."

The vehicle stopped in the drive outside, lights flashing. Two emergency medical technicians came across the porch.

Rachel met them at the door. "I'm Dr. Vale, and this is Lena Smith." She stood out of the way as one of the EMTs knelt by the couch, stethoscope in hand. "She's in ketoacidosis. I started fluids and gave her ten units of insulin."

The EMT nodded. "Got it." The two men proceeded with their standard routine and, in only a few moments, had taken Lena out on a stretcher and put her into the ambulance.

"I want to come with her," Justino said, following. "Please don't make her go alone."

The second EMT shook his head. "Not allowed. Sorry, son."

The boy staggered, as if he'd been shoved.

Garrett put a hand on his thin shoulder. "You can come with me, Justino. I'll follow the ambulance. Ford, could you call Lena's dad to let him know what's going on? Dr. Vale, I assume you want to come along, as well?" He ushered Rachel toward his truck.

"To begin with anyway. If Lena is part of this community, then I will be overseeing her care to some extent." He opened the back door for her to stow the duffel on the bench, then held the front door so she could get in.

Once in the driver's seat, he fastened his own belt and started the engine. "So today isn't a onetime emergency?"

"I'm afraid not." Rachel blew out a deep breath. "From all indications, this is a life-changing event."

"What do you mean?"

"Lena will be under a doctor's care for the rest of her life. She has juvenile-onset diabetes."

THE TRUCK TOOK a sudden leap forward, then slowed as Garrett relaxed his foot. "She'll be taking insulin shots?" He glanced at Justino in the rearview mirror. The teen was staring out the side window, lost in his own thoughts.

Rachel nodded. "Unless researchers find a cure. They're always working on it."

The prospect daunted him. "That's a real challenge for a young girl."

"The adults around her will have to help her cope. Are her parents going to be cooperative?"

"Her mother died last year. Since then, her dad has expected Lena to take care of her younger brothers and the house, as well as doing her schoolwork. She's at the ranch because she's been picked up for shoplifting several times in Buffalo and Kaycee and even Casper. She was cutting school with some of the older girls who can drive, and they'd spend the day out of town, getting into trouble. Caroline chose her for the camp, hoping it would turn her around so she could focus more on long-term goals."

"Well, now she has the long-term goal of staying healthy to worry about."

"I'll pray for her to develop the strength she needs."

"I'm sure that will help." There was no mistaking the sarcasm in her voice.

He sent her a puzzled look. "Why do you say it like that?"

She blew out a breath. "Sorry. I didn't mean to insult you."

"I'm not insulted. But I want to understand your reaction. You don't believe prayer can change events?"

"It might change the person who prays, because I believe in the power of the mind to affect behavior. But otherwise...no. Your prayer won't call down some unseen power to help Lena deal with her diabetes."

"You don't believe in God?"

She didn't answer for a minute. "I grew up going to church," she said finally. "I can't dismiss the possibility of a universal power. But as I observe life on this planet, I don't detect much evidence of any kind of divine intervention. Good or bad, what happens, happens."

There was silence as he drove the truck onto the highway exit ramp. "I'd be interested in talking more with you about that," Garrett said, once they'd merged into traffic. "Meanwhile, we'll have to work with Lena for the rest of the summer and get her started on the road to managing her condition."

The doctor shook her head. "A summer ranch camp is probably not the best place for her to do that."

Her opposition surprised him, but now wasn't the time for a debate. "We'll figure that out once she's better."

At the hospital, they pulled into the ER parking lot and went to the registration desk. Garrett showed the paperwork that granted him treatment permission, and they were allowed to join Lena in her cubicle. Justino went to the side of the bed and took hold of the girl's free hand.

"That's what you need," Rachel said, nodding at the bag of fluid hanging near Lena's head. "You'll feel better soon."

Lena rolled her head on the pillow. "I want to go back. To the ranch."

Garrett faced her from the end of the bed. "We'll take you as soon as the doctors say it's okay," he said.

"Lying around being sick at camp is no fun."

People wearing scrubs came and went, asking the girl questions and drawing blood for tests. A nurse brought some food and urged Lena to eat a little. Finally, a man wearing a white coat over his scrubs entered the cubicle, a medical chart held in one hand.

He nodded at Garrett but then shifted his attention to Rachel. "Dr. Vale? I'm Brad Stevens, from the medicine service. I understand you're the new doc down in Bisons Creek."

She gave him one of those bright smiles. "I just pulled in to town today."

"And ended up at work. That's the way it goes, doesn't it? Good call on the diagnosis." Then he moved forward to stand beside the bed. "Hi, Lena. I'm Dr. Stevens. We've run some tests and I have some news."

Lena opened her eyes to focus on his face. "What's wrong?"

"You've haven't been well for a few days, have you?" Lena shook her head. "Well, that's because your blood glucose is very high."

"I don't understand."

"Your cells use the glucose, or sugar, in the food you eat to produce energy and to function normally. There's a chemical in your body called insulin, made by the pancreas, which helps release glucose into the cells so it can be used. But sometimes there's not enough insulin. The glucose doesn't get into the cells and instead stays in your blood. Your cells are starved and you become sick."

"How do I get better?"

"We're giving you insulin, and that will make a big difference."

"Then I can leave?"

"Not right away. We want to watch you for a couple of days, ensure your system returns to a more normal state. And we have to talk about the changes you'll need to make to manage your health. You see, Lena, your condition is known as diabetes. And you'll have it for the rest of your life."

Tears welled up in Lena's big brown eyes and spilled over to run down her cheeks. "My mother had diabetes. She died."

Rachel stepped up beside Dr. Stevens to put a hand on the blanket over Lena's knee. "But that doesn't have to happen, sweetie." Her tone was gentle but reassuring. "You're going to learn how to control your condition so you can be happy and healthy and live a long, wonderful life."

"Can other people catch this diabetes from me?" Lena looked at Justino.

"Don't worry, it's not that kind of disease." Dr. Stevens closed the chart. "First, we're going to get you feeling better, then we'll explain how you can keep yourself that way. I'll talk with you again in a little while." He left the cubicle.

A moment later, a nurse parted the curtains. "Lena's father is here."

Garrett led the way to the waiting room, where a Hispanic man in work clothes came toward them. "Lena is sick?" he said. "What's wrong?"

"This is Dr. Vale," Garrett told him. "She's the new doctor in Bisons Creek and she can explain—"

"No, you are responsible for Lena," Mr. Smith interrupted. "You explain."

"Let's sit down." Garrett led the way to three chairs. "Lena has diabetes," he said when they were seated. "Like your wife."

Mr. Smith's expression didn't change. "She is going to die?"

"No," Rachel said. "She can get treatment that will keep her alive for a long time. But she will have to take care of herself."

He didn't respond to her. "How did this happen?" he demanded, glaring at Garrett. "You are supposed to keep her safe."

"This is not something anyone could predict or prevent." Garrett braced his elbows on his knees and gripped his hands together. "But we can work with Lena as she learns to handle her condition."

Mr. Smith nodded. "You will see that she knows what to do."

"Yes, but *you* should also understand—"

The other man stood up. "No. You are responsible. I signed papers. You will make sure she gets well and can do what is necessary when she comes home. That is what must happen."

Without allowing Garrett to utter another word, Lena's dad stalked out of the waiting room toward the parking lot.

"He didn't go in to visit her," Rachel said in a hollow voice.

"No." Garrett wiped a hand over his face. "And he treated you with disrespect. I'm sorry about that."

She shrugged. "He doesn't seem to value women very highly."

"I guess not. It's no wonder Lena was getting into trouble. She was crying out for attention."

"A kid needs her parents at a time like this," Rachel said fiercely. "Who's going to look after this abandoned teenaged girl?"

Garrett swallowed hard. "You heard her father. He made me responsible."

But the doctor shook her head. "Being a teenager with diabetes is tough—physically, mentally and emotionally. Lena has to have a stable support system to help her understand the healthy life she should try to live. You can't possibly accomplish that on a ranch in the middle of a summer camp!"

Chapter Two

Spine straight, shoulders square, Garrett met her gaze with narrowed eyes. "I think you're jumping to conclusions. With your help—"

"Even with my help," Rachel said before he could finish, "it would be quite a challenge, especially when you have so many kids to deal with. These first few weeks are going to be confusing for Lena, but also very important. She'll have to absorb a lot of information very quickly."

"I'm sure there are resources available. We do get the internet out here in the wild, wild West." His grin invited her to smile with him.

But she didn't cooperate. "Lena will need appointments with a team of doctors and nurses who'll supervise her treatment on a regular basis. That's a significant time commitment."

He shrugged. "There's no other option. Without a family, who else will take care of her?"

"That's for us to figure out." Rachel got to her feet. "For the moment, let's see how she's doing."

In the emergency room cubicle, Lena looked better— her eyes had brightened and a rosy color tinted her cheeks. "Where's my dad?"

Garrett cleared his throat. "We talked, but he couldn't stay."

"He doesn't handle it when other people are sick." The girl shook her head. "He wouldn't pay attention to my mother, either. And he wasn't at the hospital when she passed."

"Well, I'm here," the minister said after a stunned pause. "Dr. Vale is here. And you're getting better. That's good enough for me."

Later in the afternoon, Lena was moved to a bed in the acute care ward of the hospital. Dr. Stevens reappeared when she had settled in. "Sorry about all the tests," he said. "We have to acquire as much information as possible so we can plan your treatment." He brought forward a woman with short white-blond hair who'd accompanied him into the room. "This is Kim Kaiser. She's a nurse who specializes in diabetes education. She'll help you understand how to deal with diabetes."

"You should sit in on this," Rachel told Garrett. "If you're responsible for her, you have to understand her medications."

He made a wry face. "I'm suddenly wishing I'd paid more attention in biology class."

Kim's visit lasted about an hour. She explained the cause of diabetes, much as Dr. Stevens had done, but then proceeded to discuss the treatment, which would involve Lena taking enough insulin through the day to balance her blood sugar. Fortunately, she'd brought printed materials along, and Rachel loaned Garrett a pen so he could make notes on the pages.

"The doctors are still working out what kind of insulin you'll need," Kim told Lena. "So I'll be back tomorrow and we can go over that. But are there any questions you want to ask now?"

Lena nodded. "Is that all I have to do, take pills?" She glanced at Justino. "That doesn't seem so hard."

"I'm sorry to say that insulin can't be made into pills," Kim said. "It's a liquid that has to be injected under your skin. With a needle."

"Shots?" Lena's dark eyes went round with horror. "I have to take shots?"

Justino looked equally distressed. "She hates needles."

Kim took the protests in stride. "Then maybe you will want to use an insulin pump, which is similar to the IV you have right now. With a pump, the needle goes in once and stays for several days."

"For how long? How long do I have to do this?"

"For the rest of your life, Lena." A gentle voice, but a harsh piece of news.

The girl shook her head. "I can't. No way."

With a glance at Rachel, Garrett took a deep breath and stepped over to the bed. "Try not to get upset, Lena." He grabbed the end rail with both hands. "We'll figure out how to make it all work for you. Maybe the pump is what you need. Or…or maybe you'll have to get used to taking shots. But not right this minute. Right this minute all you have to do is relax."

She glared at him through the tears running down her cheeks. "It isn't fair!"

He shook his head. "No, it's not. You shouldn't have to deal with diabetes. Nobody should." He shrugged. "But it's happened. And in the long run you will be happiest and be able to enjoy your life if you learn to take care of yourself."

Lena had broken into sobs. Justino put his arms around her but looked at Garrett. "I think she wants to be by herself."

"We'll step out for a few minutes." He picked up his hat, held the door for Kim and Rachel, and then followed them into the hall. "I guess you have to expect an emotional reaction. It's a pretty serious diagnosis."

"Yes, it is." Kim gave him a calm smile. "As her father—"

He cleared his throat. "I'm not her dad. I'm acting in his place."

"Oh." Her brows drew together as she turned to Rachel. "Are you her mother?"

"No, I'm the physician in Bisons Creek, where Lena lives."

"I just assumed…" The nurse took a breath. "Well, if you are Lena's guardians, you'll have to help her overcome her resistance. Her very life depends on it."

As Kim left them, Garrett rubbed the nape of his neck. "Acceptance is a hard enough lesson for an adult to learn, much less a teenager. This kind of situation poses a real test of faith."

"Faith isn't the solution here." Rachel took a deep breath, trying to curb her impatience at his approach to the problem. "We have to convince her that medical science can't be ignored. It's a fact that she has diabetes, a fact that she has to take insulin or suffer serious consequences. Faith won't change those facts. There's no other reasonable choice."

His brows drew together in a worried frown. "Easier said than done."

"It is a daunting prospect." His obvious concern softened her mood, and she put her hand on his upper arm. "But you'll take it a day at a time. An hour at a time."

The frown cleared and then he smiled at her. "That's all we ever have to manage, in fact. This moment. Thanks for reminding me."

For a moment, she returned his smile, surrendering to the attraction she'd been resisting all day.

Then she remembered his vocation and disconnected her gaze from his. "We should check on Lena. I hope she's calmed down by now."

In fact, the girl had fallen asleep, curled on her side toward Justino, who sat next to the bed, holding her hand. When Rachel and Garrett entered, he eased his fingers free and came across the room to face them.

"Tell me the truth," he said, his young face set in grim lines. "Will Lena die from this diabetes?"

When Garrett glanced at her, Rachel tilted her head to indicate that he should field the question.

"The effects of untreated diabetes can be life threatening," he told the boy. "What we have to do is convince Lena to take the medicine that will prevent those effects. It won't be easy—at first anyway. But with care she can live to be a grandmother. Or a great-grandmother!"

Justino sighed. "She has always hated getting shots at the doctor. But somehow she will manage. She's strong. And I'll help her."

Garrett gripped his shoulder. "I know you will. We'll all be on Lena's side, supporting her as she gets used to a new routine. And we have Dr. Vale here in town as an added bonus. She'll be great backup."

Justino gave Rachel one of his rare smiles. "Maybe you will be more than backup," he told her. "Maybe you will be the mother Lena doesn't have."

AFTER CALLING THE ranch to give everyone a report on Lena's condition, Garrett sat down beside Rachel in the waiting room. He leaned over and spoke in a low voice. "You look terrified."

She stared straight ahead. "I have no idea what you're talking about."

"When Justino said you could be the mother Lena lost. You went pale."

"I was startled, that's all. Teenagers are usually more suspicious of adults."

"I think these two are grabbing at whatever resources they can reach. You're going to be one of them."

Her expression relaxed slightly. "I'm glad to be Lena's doctor. But I can't step in as her mother. There's a reason doctors don't treat their own family—it's called objectivity."

"Do you want kids some day?"

Now she frowned at him. "I don't know. Do you?"

He nodded. "Definitely. Kids are fun." Then he reconsidered. "But also scary. I guess I have to get past that somehow, to be useful to Lena."

"That's the point of remaining objective," Rachel said. "When you're taking care of somebody, you focus on the facts and what can be done, not the emotions involved. It's called equanimity—staying calm in the midst of a high-pressure situation. As one of my teachers suggested, 'First, take your own pulse.'"

"So that's how you doctors manage. Must take lots of practice."

"Internship and residency are all about equanimity. The more cases you see, the better your control."

Garrett cocked his head. "And you like being in control."

"Are we still talking about medicine?"

He grinned. "That's up to you."

"Well, then, I admit I'm pretty much a control freak, professionally and personally. Life runs smoother that way."

"You've never encountered circumstances you couldn't control?"

"Of course I have," she said, her tone sharp. Then she drew a deep breath. "Everybody does," she said more calmly.

"That's good. For a minute there, I thought you were perfect." When she laughed, he nodded. "There you go. I knew you'd have a great laugh."

Her lips parted in surprise, and her cheeks flushed. He wondered if he might get a flirtatious comeback.

But in the next moment, she stood up abruptly. "I'm going to stretch my legs. I'll be back in a few minutes."

Before Garrett could say another word, she'd hurried out the door.

BETWEEN A TRIP to the restroom and a walk around the entire hospital, Rachel managed to waste half an hour she might have otherwise spent sitting with Garrett Marshall. Flirting with Garrett Marshall.

Not that flirting was a skill she'd had much practice with—medical school and training hadn't left a lot of time for romance.

But Garrett wasn't someone she wanted to think of in a romantic context anyway. She wasn't going to fall for the cowboy type, no matter how ruggedly handsome he might be. Of course, Garrett was more than a cowboy. He was also a minister.

And that was the real issue between them, one that couldn't be resolved with any amount of flirting or getting better acquainted. As a pastor, Garrett Marshall counted on the effectiveness of prayer and the possibility of miracles. He led a church—a congregation of people who shared his convictions.

But during her mother's illness, Rachel had witnessed the damage such groups and their beliefs could do. In the wrong hands, religion became a tool for deception and greed. If it weren't for her unquestioning faith in a corrupt con man, Sarah Vale might still be alive. While Rachel didn't question the right of others to their devotion, she certainly didn't intend to join them.

By the time she returned to the waiting room, Lena had awakened. She was calm, though Rachel saw the fear of an uncertain future in her eyes. When her dinner arrived, she ate a few bites, which was a good sign. After a night on insulin, she would probably wake in the morning ready to finish her entire breakfast and more. Rachel said as much to Garrett on their way back to Bisons Creek.

"I'm glad to hear her appetite will improve," Garrett said. "She's always been slender, but I didn't realize until today that she was losing weight. I should have noticed."

"You wouldn't necessarily recognize the signs," Rachel assured him. "Unless something brought it to your attention."

"I hate leaving Lena in the hospital alone," Justino said from the backseat. "She looked so scared."

Garrett blew out a breath. "I know. But she's got the television for a diversion. She'll probably fall asleep pretty fast."

"Can we go see her early in the morning?"

"We'll leave after breakfast."

Though Rachel didn't have her bearings yet about locations in and around Bisons Creek, she was surprised when Garrett turned onto the Circle M Ranch drive before taking her to the clinic. He stopped the truck at the house to let Justino out.

"Miss Caroline will have saved you some dinner," he told the boy. "Try to take it easy tonight and not worry too much. Lena's being well cared for and she's getting better."

"I hope so."

"He doesn't sound convinced." Garrett drove back toward the ranch entrance. "I guess I can't blame him."

"He would have stayed with her all night if you had let him," Rachel said. "They're very close for such a young couple." She paused for a moment. "Did you want to talk to me about something? You could have dropped me off first."

He shrugged one shoulder. "It occurred to me that neither of us has had lunch or dinner. I thought maybe you'd be interested in getting something to eat."

"Oh." The suggestion should have been simple enough, except for the combination of excitement and reluctance ambushing her brain. Garrett Marshall was way too appealing for her to spend a lot of time with. The last thing she wanted to do was get closer to him.

"Is that a yes or a no?"

Still, she was hungry. "Um, okay. Sure. Food sounds like a good idea."

"Great. We've got a diner here in town—the only restaurant, actually—where the cooking is really excellent. You might as well get familiar with it on your first day here."

"It is still my first day, isn't it?" She sighed. "I haven't even unpacked the car. Or gone to my apartment. That's the way medicine is sometimes."

"We appreciate your being here for what was clearly an emergency." He pulled the truck into a parking space beside a building with the sign Kate's Diner. Then he looked over in the dim light and grinned. "The least I can do is buy you dinner on your first night in town."

Alarms went off in Rachel's head—he made it sound way too much like a date. But she could hardly retreat at this point. Maybe she could talk him into splitting the check.

Garrett opened the door for her, a courtesy that upped her discomfort level. Then he pulled out a chair at the table and invited her to sit. Short of staging a fight, there wasn't much she could do other than take the seat he offered.

She met his gaze directly as he sat down across the table. "This isn't a date."

His eyebrows rose. "Not technically. No."

That response didn't reassure her. "Not even remotely."

He folded his arms on the table. "Would it be such a bad idea?"

"We aren't a couple. Aren't *going* to be a couple."

"That's a pretty sweeping prediction. We only met this morning. Do you dislike me so much already?"

She had to tell the truth. "No, of course not. But the two of us are incompatible."

"I disagree. I think we've had a good day together."

A pretty, brown-haired woman came to their table. "Hey, Garrett. Long time no see."

"Hi, Terri. Yeah, we've been pretty busy out on the ranch with the kids plus the regular chores. Let me introduce you to the newest citizen in town—this is Dr. Rachel Vale. She'll be operating the Bisons Creek Medical Clinic."

Terri's face brightened. "I heard we were getting a doctor. Welcome! It will be so great to be able to visit a clinic in town when one of the kids has an ear infection instead of driving half an hour just to get a prescription."

Rachel smiled. "I'm glad to be here. I look forward to helping you out when you need medical advice."

"I'll be sure to call. But for right now, what can I get you two to drink?"

"Water," she and Garrett both said at the same time.

"Got it." Terri scribbled on her notepad. "We still have some of the special available, which is meat loaf with mashed potatoes and gravy and Kate's slow-cooked green beans. I'll be back in a minute to take your orders."

"So," Garrett said when the server had left, "you were going to tell me why we're incompatible."

"We have different worldviews." Rachel clasped her hands on the table. "As a minister, you operate on the assumption that faith will make things right. But as a doctor, I use science and facts to deal with the world."

Terri reappeared with a glass of water for each of them. "And what will you have to eat?"

Once they both ordered the meat loaf, Rachel resumed her explanation. "People with such opposite perspectives can't find common ground for a relationship."

Laughter sparked in his blue eyes. "Are you hoping to persuade me or yourself?"

She glared at him. "You're awfully sure I'm attracted to you, aren't you?"

"I wasn't, till you started trying to convince me we can't go on a simple date."

"There's nothing simple about dating."

"So you've had some bad experiences?"

"Hasn't everybody had a bad date?"

"Sure. A few years ago, I went out with a woman who brought her grandmother along with us to dinner."

Rachel had to laugh. "You're kidding, right?"

"At first, I figured her grandmother just wanted to check me out. But when Nana showed up for the second go-round, I decided I'd had enough of the two-for-one program."

"I'm not surprised."

"Especially since Nana monopolized every conversation with details of her surgical adventures."

"Oh, no."

"Can you top that?"

"I don't think so. Most of my bad dates were with guys who thought buying dinner entitled them to play doctor afterward."

"Rude." He waited while Terri set their plates down and left again. "I promise to keep my hands to myself." After a moment, he winked. "Tonight."

Rachel frowned at him. "You're a problem."

They ate in silence for a few minutes, giving the delicious food the appreciation it deserved. "At least now I know where to come for a decent meal," she said when her hunger had been eased. "I don't have to depend on peanut-butter-and-jelly sandwiches."

"You're not a cook?"

"I can make a salad, boil pasta or bake a potato in the microwave. Being a doctor hasn't offered much opportunity to develop complex cooking skills."

"So what do you do on your days off?"

"There haven't been many of those. But I usually go for a run if I've got an hour of daylight. And I like to read."

Garrett grinned at her. "See, we do have something in common. I like to read, too. What do you read?"

"Not religious texts."

"We were talking about free time. And you're determined to pigeonhole me, aren't you?"

She pushed her empty plate away. "I'm a doctor. That role defines my whole life. You're a minister. Wouldn't you say the same?"

"But you're also a runner and a reader. And probably a few other things I've yet to discover. I'm a minister, yes, but I also work on a ranch. I rode bucking broncs in the rodeo. I volunteer with at-risk kids. I'm a brother and soon to be a brother-in-law to a friend of yours. Do you have family?"

Rachel swallowed hard. "No."

He studied her for a moment, his eyes narrowed. "You lost somebody recently."

She shook her head. "Not so recent. My mom died two years ago."

"I'm sorry." His voice was gentle. "You still miss her."

Just like that, tears stung her eyes. For something to do, Rachel picked up her glass and took a long swallow of water. Blinking hard, she said, "Sorry. I must be tired."

"No problem. Losing a parent is tough. If you ever want to talk about it, I'll be glad to listen."

"That's okay." She sent him a forced smile. "I'm fine."

"Dessert?" Terri asked, appearing suddenly beside them. "We've got fresh lemon meringue pie."

The idea of so much sugar after a day spent dealing with diabetes didn't appeal to Rachel. "Just some coffee, please."

"Me, too," Garrett said. "Then I'll help you get your car unloaded."

"No, please," Rachel started. "I can manage—"

"But it will go faster with two people working at it." He winked again. "You can't get rid of me. You might as well give in."

"Then you can let me take care of dinner." When Terri put the check on the table, Rachel managed to get her fingers on it first. "So there."

He raised his hands in a gesture of surrender. "I recognize when resistance is futile. But I will get even."

Darkness had fallen before they arrived at the clinic. Rachel stared through the truck window at the building she'd visited only briefly this morning. "Seems like days ago I arrived." She blew out a deep breath and turned to Garrett. "You should go home."

"Soon. You don't even know where your apartment is, do you?"

"Sure I do. Evans Street."

"How do you get there from here?"

"Caroline sent me a map…"

"Just get in your vehicle and let me lead the way. You can worry about maps tomorrow."

Suddenly too tired to protest, Rachel did as she was instructed. In five minutes, they pulled up at the curb in front of an older two-story house with a wraparound porch.

Garrett came to her window. "This is it. You've got Caroline for an upstairs neighbor, though she's not here much this summer. Luckily, the first-floor tenant moved out just at the right moment to give you a home."

"It seems to be a nice place." She pulled the key she'd been sent out of her purse. "So far, so good."

The interior was cozy, filled with secondhand furniture that appeared comfortable, if a little dated and dusty. The kitchen was bigger than Rachel would need, the bathroom smaller than she would have preferred. "This will work for me," she said as she and Garrett approached her car. "Compared to the places I lived during med school, it's a palace."

He pulled a couple of suitcases out of the back of the SUV. "We make sacrifices when we really want something, don't we?"

She didn't answer because it disturbed her that he understood what she'd been through without having to be told. He was altogether too easy to talk to, too perceptive and too easygoing. It would be better if he got angry or at least annoyed when she resisted him. Instead, he just smiled.

In a few short minutes, all the belongings she'd labored to fit into her vehicle were set in convenient places around her new apartment. Garrett put the last box of books on the coffee table and straightened. "Do you have more stuff coming?"

"No, this is it. I got rid of a lot of things before I left Seattle. I wanted to start new here."

"An admirable plan." He put his hands in his pockets. "I should leave and let you settle in. Thanks again for helping out with Lena today—it made a big difference to have a doctor available to deal with this crisis. You're going to be a real benefit to this community."

"I'm glad I could help." She followed him as he walked to the door. "Thank you for helping carry all this inside. It would have taken me a lot longer. And I'm pretty tired."

"My pleasure." He faced her at the door. "Justino and I will be heading to the hospital in the morning. Can I pick you up?"

"I'm meeting with my new nurse early tomorrow," she said, determined to set some limits. "But I'll check on Lena as soon as possible. I'm sure the doctors on staff have her condition under control. I've applied for privileges at the hospital, but I'm not currently Lena's doctor. And—" she gave him a pointed look "—I'm not her family."

"Of course. It's just been such a relief to have someone around who really understands what's happening." His serious blue gaze captured hers. "Your support meant a lot to me today."

The hall light was dim, and they stared at each other in the shadows. The moment seemed more intimate than it should, more important.

"Good night, Rachel Vale," he said finally, his voice low.

"Good night, Garrett Marshall." She wanted to break the connection between them but couldn't quite seem to do it.

Then he bent forward and kissed her on the cheek. The press of his lips burned like a brand. "Sleep well." His boot heels thudded on the porch floor as he walked quickly away.

Rachel didn't watch him drive off. That would be foolish and romantic, neither of which she intended to be. She was practical and logical, she told herself as she went into the bedroom, rational and pragmatic.

Rummaging through her overnight bag for pajamas and a toothbrush, she assured herself that there wasn't a mark on her cheek from that kiss, and proved it when she went into the bathroom and turned on the light over the sink.

But she could still feel his lips on her cheek when she put her head on the pillow and tried to fall asleep.

Chapter Three

Garrett found himself whistling while he drove home. He recognized the tune as a love song by one of his favorite artists and grinned.

Not that he had fallen in love. Not yet. But all day long, even through the worry and distress over Lena, he had been aware of an effervescence in the air, a sense of excitement and anticipation he could only relate to Rachel Vale. Even when she gave him those cute frowns of hers, he wanted to smile. He appreciated her caring approach to Lena's very real fears and her calm expertise in the face of a crisis. Her direct refusal to consider their dinner a date appealed to his sense of fairness. At least he knew where he stood with her.

He had to agree that their relationship would be complicated. His faith was the foundation of his life, and Rachel's skepticism presented a serious obstacle. Garrett suspected the reason for her resistance had something to do with her mother's death. He hoped she would confide in him about that reason and let him help her deal with her grief.

He would have to earn her trust to make that happen, a task he looked forward to with pleasure. Setting up in a new town, Rachel would no doubt feel isolated, maybe even lonely. Bringing her into the community, into his circle of friends and family, would be his primary goal.

As he turned onto the county road that would take him to the ranch, Garrett blinked hard at the sudden vision in his mind's eye—Rachel and him as a couple, serving Christmas day dinner to the guests at the shelter in Casper, alongside a couple of red-haired kids. Their kids.

The image stopped his heart for a second. That kind of family—mom, dad and kids—had disappeared from his life when he was twelve years old. His memories from before that time were few, but he could recall an afternoon at the county fair. He had ridden the roller coaster with his dad and Wyatt and Ford while his mother held baby Dylan. He'd eaten cotton candy, visited the animal barns and the craft exhibits, ending the day with a ride on the Ferris wheel. Without a doubt, the day had been one of the best of his life.

Something about Rachel Vale had dredged up that sense of joy. Maybe it was her gentleness with Lena, or a certain sweetness in her smile. Beautiful, intelligent, dependable and devoted to her patients—now that he considered the matter, the lovely lady doctor struck him as the perfect woman with whom to build the kind of family he'd been missing for more than twenty years.

Garrett shook his head. "Slow down, man," he said aloud, driving under the sign for the ranch. "You don't even have the horse and the cart in the same county, let alone one in front of the other."

First, Rachel would have to relax her guard, accept him as a person she could rely on. Not to mention resolving the small matter of her resistance to the fundamentals of his job description.

Then…if she shared this powerful attraction he'd

experienced all day...*then* they could investigate this falling-in-love business. Together.

When he parked the truck near the ranch house, he realized that tonight had been designated a homemade ice cream event. All the teenagers—except for Lena—were gathered on the front porch with bowls in their hands. Caroline and Ford sat in rocking chairs with their own servings.

Caroline got to her feet as he came up the steps. "Perfect timing. Let me get you some ice cream."

He put up hand. "No thanks. Not tonight." After a day spent worrying about Lena's blood-sugar levels, the thought of a sweet dessert didn't hold much appeal.

She stared at him with a worried frown, since he always enjoyed their ice-cream concoctions. "Are you okay?"

"Sure. How's everybody here?" He noticed Justino sitting on the corner of the porch, focused on his phone. "Did he get dinner?"

"He didn't really want anything, but I convinced him to finish half a burger and some salad. And he did eat his dessert." She sighed. "He's been texting constantly since he got here. I didn't have the heart to cut him off. Lena must be so scared."

"The nurses are taking care of her. She ate some dinner and was feeling much better when we left."

Ford stepped up and put a hand on his shoulder. "I'm guessing you had a pretty hard day."

"I just stood around. Lena's the one with the illness." Garrett opened the screen door and led the way into the living room, for a less exposed conversation. "Did you reassure the rest of the kids?"

"We explained that she was getting better but didn't

define the exact problem." Ford gave a slight shrug. "We weren't really sure how to deal with that."

Garrett shook his head. "Me, neither. Teenagers hate being different. And Lena's pretty image conscious. I'll have to talk with her about what she wants everybody to know. Though, really, I don't believe we can keep it quiet. We all live pretty close together here."

"The whole situation is going to be complicated," Ford said. "Just making ice cream will challenge Lena's new lifestyle. But the others will be disappointed if we don't continue the events." He paused for a moment. "I'm wondering if the best thing wouldn't be for Lena to be at home as she learns to adapt—fewer distractions and temptations in an environment she can control."

"Not at all." He hadn't discussed his conversation with Mr. Smith over the telephone, but he described it to Ford and Caroline now. "He basically abandoned Lena to my care. So, ready or not, I'm her support system. *We* are her support system. We'll have to figure out how to help her adjust."

"Mr. Garrett?" Becky Rush and Lizzie Hanson, the other two girls in the camp, stood at the front door. "Can we come in?"

"Sure. How are you tonight? Did you have a good afternoon?"

Becky, a redhead with freckles, nodded. "We went for a long trail ride to part of the ranch we hadn't seen before."

"We came to a pond," Lizzie added. "Deep Pond, is that right?" She looked at Caroline, who smiled. "There was a whole herd of deer grazing in the grass. They stared at us for a long time and then bolted into the trees. They were beautiful."

"They had fawns with them," Becky said. "Pretty big ones, but they still had white spots."

"We wanted to ask about Lena." Lizzie played with the ends of her blond hair, not meeting Garrett's gaze. "When can she come back?"

"It'll be a couple of days," he said. "She has to learn how to take some medicine when she leaves the hospital, so they'll be helping her with that new routine. But soon enough we'll have her here again."

Becky swallowed hard. "It was scary when she fell. I was afraid she hurt herself."

"We all were," Caroline said. "But this was a problem that had been getting worse for her over a period of days or weeks, not something that suddenly happened."

"And nobody else will get sick?" Lizzie asked, cheeks flushing bright red under her makeup.

"Nobody else can get sick," Garrett assured her. "Don't worry."

"I want her to get well."

"We all do."

Having asked their main question, the girls returned to the porch.

"I'll discuss this with Lena tomorrow," Garrett said. "And advise her that giving the other teens the whole truth is the best idea. I promised Justino we'd go to the hospital after breakfast."

Ford shifted his balance, a familiar sign of irritation. "We need you here, too. These six kids deserve attention. Then there's ranch work to do, and Wyatt's a long way from being ready. Dylan's spending more of his day in the studio working on his sculpture. Caroline and I both have jobs in town that we've been neglecting."

"And I have a church to take care of." Garrett pulled in

a deep breath. "I understand that we're all stretched to the limit. I'll do the best I can to be in three places at once."

"We all will," Caroline said, easing the tension. "Did you like Rachel? I loved how she dealt with Lena."

"She's great." He was careful not to sound too enthusiastic. "Having her at the hospital made everything much easier. And I think Lena already understands she can depend on Dr. Vale."

"I imagine we'll be depending on Dr. Vale quite a bit ourselves," Ford said. "We'll require someone to help us cope with Lena's condition. None of us is remotely educated."

"I'm sure Rachel will provide great backup." Which would, luckily, give him a chance to know her better. "I did pick up some information at the hospital this afternoon when the nurse talked to Lena about insulin. And tonight I'm going to research diabetes more on the internet."

Ford shook his head. "You're not her parent, Garrett. You can't manage this as if you were."

"Her dad consigned her to my care. What else can I do?"

Caroline put a hand on his arm. "We'll work it out, Garrett. All of us together will support you and Lena through this."

He put his palm over her fingers. "Thanks. Between the Marshalls—you included, Caroline—and Rachel Vale, Lena's got the best family available."

But the next morning, Garrett wasn't sure even the Marshalls and Rachel Vale would be enough. When he and Justino arrived at Lena's room, Kim Kaiser was there. And Lena was in tears.

"No, no, no," she wailed. "I can't."

Justino rushed to the bed. "What's wrong?"

She threw herself against his chest. "I can't give myself shots. It hurts!"

Kim stood calmly on the other side, with a syringe and other equipment laid out on a cloth. She glanced at Garrett. "This isn't unusual. It's a pretty challenging prospect, giving yourself a shot. But—" she moved her gaze to Lena "—it has to be done."

"Even with the insulin pump?"

"The pump portal has to be changed, which is similar to an injection." As the sobs continued, Kim moved her equipment to a nearby table. "I'll give her a few minutes," she said and left the room.

As if Rachel were there to tell him so, Garrett knew he had to respond rationally to help Lena calm down. She was a high-spirited, emotional girl. But she would have to exercise some logic in order to save her own life. Still, there was something to be said for the empathetic approach he'd learned as a minister. Maybe the two could work together...

He waited until she quieted and reclined again on her pillow, still holding tightly to Justino's hand. "I can understand how upsetting this is," Garrett told her. "Why would you deliberately stick yourself with a needle?"

Lena sniffed. "I hate shots. Since I was little."

"Here's the thing, though." He'd stayed up reading and now had a good grasp on the facts. "Your blood sugar will change during the day depending on what you eat but also on what you're doing and other factors you can't even control. Because your body isn't monitoring that level for you, you have to do it yourself. Sometimes your blood sugar will be low, and you'll need to eat. Sometimes it will be high and you'll need insulin."

He paused and made sure he had her attention. "The thing is, if you want to stay well—to feel good and do the things you enjoy, including being with Justino and your friends—you must take injections. Now, you can find somebody to do that for you—me, for instance. But that would mean finding me, interrupting whatever I'm doing, pulling up your shirt or pulling down your pants so I can inject you."

"No!"

"Or you can take responsibility for your health. Learn to accept that this is something you have to do to take care of yourself, like brushing your teeth."

As Lena gazed at him, tears flowed down her cheeks. "I don't want to."

Garrett put a hand over hers. "I know. And I'm sorry. But it's necessary in order to keep you happy and alive."

When Kim returned, Lena was resigned, though far from cheerful. "I guess I have to do this," she said. "But I hate it."

"You'll get used to it," the nurse reassured her. "Eventually it'll be no big deal." She moved her equipment back to the side of the bed. "Now, here's what you'll do."

Garrett drew Justino out of the room with him, to give Lena privacy. "It's a hard thing," the boy said. "I can't stand that she has to suffer this way."

Another parental moment. Garrett sighed silently. "But if you are going to help Lena manage her health, you can't feel sorry her. You have to be brave so she can be brave. Does that make sense?"

The boy heaved a deep breath. "I guess so. I can try."

"Lena's dad isn't much help." Garrett decided to be honest. "So you and I and Dr. Vale are going to be her team. Her cheerleaders. Can you do that? For Lena?"

Justino nodded decisively. "I can."

"Good job." The voice coming from behind him was Rachel's.

Garrett pivoted to face her. "I didn't realize you'd arrived."

"I didn't want to interrupt your conversation, but I couldn't help overhearing." She smiled at Justino. "Garrett is right. You can be a big help to Lena. I'm sure she'll appreciate your encouragement with the changes she'll be making in her life."

"I'll do my best."

"I know you will. For you," she said to Garrett, "I brought books." She held out a couple of volumes, one a thin paperback but the other quite a hefty load. "The big one is more of an encyclopedia—don't try to read it cover to cover. The smaller one is about coping with diabetic teenagers. I unpacked the boxes in my office this morning and there they were."

"Thanks." In the midst of a serious medical situation, he could still notice how her shirt matched the blue of her eyes, how her khaki slacks showed off a small waist and rounded hips, how her russet hair caught the light. "Did you have a restful night?"

"It was fine." She didn't meet his eyes. "How's Lena this morning?"

Garrett related Lena's response to the prospect of injections and how he'd handled it. "She agreed to cooperate, at least."

"I'm afraid it's going to take more toughness on your part and Lena's to succeed." Her voice was cool, her expression distant, as if she didn't want to be talking with him.

Kim Kaiser came out of the hospital room. "I'm giving Lena a break, a chance to absorb what I've showed her. This afternoon we can all go over what she's learned. Will that work for everyone?"

"Sure."

Justino immediately went inside to be with Lena. Garrett watched the nurse make her way down the hall and then looked back at Rachel. "Having second thoughts?"

She was watching Kim retreat down the hallway. "I beg your pardon?"

"My guess is that you woke up this morning and decided that you let me get too close last night. So today you're making sure to put space between us, so I won't get the wrong idea."

When her startled gaze came to his, he gave her a quizzical smile. "Do you really think that's going to work?"

RACHEL DIDN'T LIKE being so easily read. "Why would you come to mind at all this morning?" She made herself hold his stare, but she could feel heat rising in her cheeks.

"For the same reason you came to my mind. Simple attraction."

She restrained herself from rushing into denial, which would only confirm his suspicion. "That's a pretty big assumption. We only met yesterday."

"But we spent most of the day together—several dates' worth of time, in my estimation. I believe I know you pretty well already."

"I doubt that. And I'm sure I don't know you."

"Evidently well enough to declare that we're incompatible."

"That's based on one obvious fact."

"Which to me makes it a pretty shaky conclusion. As a rational person, shouldn't you investigate further and determine whether you're right or whether you might, in actuality, be wrong? We could be the most well-matched couple in Bisons Creek. And that's saying something, since we have married folks approaching their fiftieth wedding anniversary."

Rachel shook her head. "You're persistent, I'll give you that. But why put ourselves through the pain of trying out a relationship that simply can't succeed? I'm going to be busy establishing my practice. You have your church, your ranch, the teenagers you're working with and now Lena's diabetes. Neither of us has time to wedge another person into our lives, especially when that person will only make trouble."

"Make trouble?"

"I'll get impatient with your faith-based approach to life. You'll try to change my mind, draw me into your church, which I'll resist. We'll argue and then we'll break up, with a lot of torment on both sides. I'm suggesting we avoid that distress by keeping our connection casual."

His smile faded and he gave a long, low whistle. "You've got it all figured out, after one day." Hands in the pockets of his jeans, he shrugged. "I think you're wrong about both of us. As I see it, we could learn from each other, improve both our lives by sharing our points of view. I'm not some wild-eyed hermit who sees visions and hears voices. I'm just an ordinary guy who hopes to make things better for the people of his community with a little faith, hope and love. And the greatest of those is love." He sighed. "If casual is what you want, though, that's what you'll get. Ready to check in with Lena?"

"Of course."

He let her go into the room ahead of him, his usual polite approach. But Rachel noticed a difference in the air around them, as if a light had dimmed and there were shadows where there used to be brightness. Garrett seemed to be himself when talking to Lena and Justino, telling jokes and relating stories about his adventures on the ranch. He was certainly as polite as ever when she joined in the conversation. But the coolness of his gaze when he glanced at her, his politeness as he listened when she spoke, put a chill in the air. She wished she had a sweater to warm up.

Kim Kaiser returned in the afternoon to give Lena and Garrett an intensive session on insulin—the different types and how to measure it, the kinds of situations that called for adjustments in dosages.

Lena soon got frustrated. "This is worse than school! I can't understand all these numbers and names."

Garrett was frowning at the papers he'd been given. "I have to agree. Rapid-acting, intermediate, long-term… how do we know what to use when?"

Kim obviously tried to be patient. "Lena will test her blood-sugar level and then decide how much insulin to take based on what she has eaten or is planning to eat."

"How often do I have to do this test?"

"When you get up in the morning, before lunch, before dinner and at bedtime."

"Every day?"

"That would be safest. Another positive step to take is a twenty-four-hour check, so you'll track how your blood sugar behaves during the night when you're asleep."

"That sounds pretty difficult," Garrett said. "Setting an alarm every couple of hours?"

"Or having someone wake her up to do the test."

Lena slapped her hands down on the blanket. "Wonderful."

Rachel walked to the end of the bed. "This all seems overwhelming, doesn't it?"

"Oh, yes."

"There's a lot you have to learn at the beginning. As with any new skill—horses, for example. You didn't just get on and know everything about riding."

"It was easier than this."

"Or how about dancing? Do you like to dance? Salsa, maybe?"

Lena glanced at her boyfriend and grinned. "We love to dance."

"But you had to learn the steps slowly at first, and concentrate on where to put each foot, how to move your hips and hands and head."

"I guess so."

"With your diabetes, you have to learn the steps. Testing your blood sugar is the first one. Knowing which insulin to take at the right time is next. Figuring out when and what to eat is also important. All of these moves will help you stay well."

"But it's *sooooo* complicated."

"Salsa dancing is complicated for me," Garrett said. "I'm totally uncoordinated when I try."

That made Lena laugh, as he'd surely intended. "I can teach you," she said, "when we go back."

"It's a plan." He nodded firmly. "But for now, we have to concentrate on insulin."

When Kim left the room later in the afternoon, Lena had gained a basic understanding of her routine. "I won't be able to do anything but testing and taking shots," she pouted. "I'll never get to have fun anymore."

"Yes, you will," Rachel said. "Because, as happens with dancing, you'll get faster at testing, injecting and managing your supplies."

"There is one more thing we need to talk about." Garrett took a chair at the side of the bed. "Caroline and Ford reassured the other kids at the ranch that you were getting better and the doctors were taking care of you. The question is, do you want them to know you have diabetes? We could explain what that means, kind of prepare them for the fact that you'll be testing and taking injections. It's your decision but, in my opinion, that would be easiest."

Lena let her head rest against the pillow, and tears seeped from underneath her closed eyelids. "It's not enough to have to deal with this. I have to be embarrassed in front of everyone, too."

"Nobody will care, Lena." Justino took her hand. "They won't think different of you."

Rachel nodded. "Everybody has limitations. Garrett can't dance."

"Hey, I can do a nice two-step. It's just that salsa thing I don't get."

"I can't sing," Rachel continued, ignoring him. "Much as I would enjoy it, my voice croaks like a frog. Your limitation is that you have to manage your blood sugar because your body won't do it automatically. That's all. It's really a simple problem, and not the worst one you could have. You're a strong girl who can handle this well if she puts her mind to it."

The room was quiet for a few minutes while Lena wrestled with the new facts of her life. Rachel found herself gazing at Garrett but shifted her focus when he glanced in her direction. The less contact between them, the easier it would be to let whatever wanted to develop die.

"I guess you'd better tell them," Lena said finally, with a sigh. "If they don't want to be around me, at least I'll know why."

"Good choice." Garrett patted her shoulder. "Everybody has been worried about you, so hearing the truth will comfort them. And I bet you'll find your friendships are the same as before. You're no different—you just have a few extra things to consider."

Rachel considered that assessment too optimistic, but

decided not to put a damper on the moment. "You'll regain your balance," she assured the girl. "There are lots of professional athletes and Hollywood stars who live successfully with diabetes. You can, too."

A nurse knocked on the door and then entered, carrying a food tray. "Dinnertime," she said. "Do try to eat as much as you can."

Garrett got to his feet. "We'll leave you alone for a few minutes. Then we have to head back to the Circle M, Justino. We've been gone all day."

Out in the hall, he gazed at the papers in his hand. "Lena's right. This reminds me of chemistry class, where your grade depends on doing the lab exactly according to the instructions. Only it's not just a grade, it's her life."

Rachel hardened her heart against his concern. "As I said yesterday, you're taking on a formidable task. Are you sure Lena doesn't have family who could supervise her?"

"I'm sure. Caroline checked her records at the office. There's no one listed in the paperwork."

She shook her head. "Then, for better or worse, you're going to have to master the information and use it. The more you understand, the less likely you'll be to make a mistake."

He stared at her with wide eyes. "What kind of mistakes?"

"If she takes too much insulin, then she'll have to eat something to get sugar into her system. If she doesn't take enough, she'll have to test her blood and adjust the next dose. Diabetes isn't an instantaneous problem—it's a daily, weekly process of balance. With practice, you both should get used to the routine. How much longer does the ranch camp last?"

"About a month."

"So Lena has a month to absorb this process before she'll have to take care of herself without help. It's not much time."

"But it's all we get." He blew out a deep breath. "I have a feeling we'll be bothering you a lot once Lena leaves the hospital."

"In that case…" She reached into her purse and brought out a few of the business cards she had ordered. "This is the number. Take enough cards to put in various places you might call from—the kitchen, the place Lena sleeps, the barn, even. And keep your cell phone close by."

"Our cell reception is sketchy out on the ranch, but we have landlines in all those places you mentioned, so I should be able to get in touch." His mouth relaxed into a smile. "Thanks for your help."

The jump in her pulse as their eyes met was a reminder of why she should keep Garrett Marshall at a distance. She was just too susceptible to his charm. "No problem. That's what I'm in Bisons Creek to do."

There was a moment of silence, as he absorbed what she'd said. "Right. You're the town doctor. It's your job." Then he leaned through the doorway into Lena's room. "We'd better hit the road, Justino. Don't want to miss dinner again. Lena, we will see you tomorrow morning. Have a good night."

With the boy dragging reluctantly behind him, Garrett headed toward the elevator, giving Rachel a two-fingered salute off his hat brim as he passed.

Rachel realized she'd hurt his feelings, but what else could she do? He imagined possibilities where she saw only obstacles, and encouraging him would be unkind. She was absolutely convinced they would both be better off never letting anything emotional develop between them. Garrett would understand one day. If she just held firm.

She went in and sat with Lena for a little while, encouraged to note that she'd regained some appetite and had eaten a good portion of her dinner. Soon enough, though, texts to and from Justino were taking most of the girl's attention, so Rachel stood up from the chair by the bed. "I'll leave for the night. But I'll stop by tomorrow to check on how you're getting along."

Lena gave her a sweet smile. "Thank you for being here. It helps to have you and Mr. Garrett to explain things."

"I'm glad. We'll do what we can to make this new life as easy as possible for you. You're old enough to be able to take care of yourself—you just have to learn how."

Her phone buzzed again, but Lena didn't immediately read the text. "My dad expects me to take care of my brothers when I'm home."

"We'll work on your schedule so that's possible. And maybe we can get your dad to recognize the challenges you're facing so he'll lighten your load."

But Lena shook her head. "That will never happen." Another buzz on her phone distracted her. "Night," she said, and shifted her focus.

"Good night."

After leaving the hospital, Rachel stopped by the grocery store in Buffalo so she could stock the refrigerator and pantry in her new kitchen. The drive home showed her a breathtaking sunset as the clouds streaking the western sky glowed red and gold over the peaks of the Big Horn Mountains. Purple twilight shadowed the rolling plains at the base of the mountain range, adding to the rich palette of colors.

Coming back to Wyoming was a terrific choice. All

the years away, she'd missed the spectacular views in her home state.

As long as she kept her distance from Garrett Marshall.

Unloading the shopping bags and fixing something to eat kept her occupied until full dark. She unpacked some of her personal books onto the shelves in the living room, reconnecting with old favorites she hadn't enjoyed in years. She'd just chosen one to read for the night when her phone rang.

"Rachel, it's Caroline. How are you settling in?"

They chatted about the apartment for a few minutes, and Rachel reported her assessment of Lena's progress. "It's a big change for a teenager," she told her friend. "Teens think they're immortal, and finding out they have this demanding disease can really knock them for a loop. But she's going to pull it off. She's a smart girl."

"I'll be relieved when she's on the ranch again where we can look after her. Although Garrett says the information he's gotten so far is pretty challenging. I have to admit those papers don't make much sense to me."

"It's going to be difficult for all of you. We could have a meeting to go over the injection plan and her daily routine. That way everybody is on the same page."

"That would make me feel better," Caroline said. "And it brings up, in a way, the reason I called, besides just to find out how you're doing. I had a brilliant idea this afternoon."

"And what brilliant idea was that?"

"Well, I mentioned to you that we're trying to teach these kids responsibility, how to take care of themselves and make sound choices in their lives."

"Right."

"It occurred to me that one of the skills they'll need

in the future is the ability to handle minor injuries and illness. We've already had a couple of accidents that required first aid. On a ranch, people are always getting scrapes or burns or cuts. Not to mention colds and the flu."

"And so…"

"And so it occurred to me how great it would be if you could come out to the ranch and give the kids some instruction in first aid and basic home health care. Isn't that a fantastic concept?"

"Um…sure." Garrett's face flashed through Rachel's mind. So much for trying to stay out of his way.

"You could even go over CPR and the Heimlich maneuver, because you never know when that kind of emergency could come up. What do you think? Doesn't it sound terrific for the kids?"

A man's voice said something on Caroline's end, though Rachel couldn't understand the words.

Her friend chuckled. "Ford wants you to know that I make use of everybody like this, that you're not the only one I impose on. Thanks so much for the support, dear," she told her fiancé. "So what would be good for your schedule?" she asked Rachel. "When can we start?"

Caroline's gung-ho enthusiasm was familiar to Rachel from their college days. "I can probably come out around lunchtime, since I doubt I'll have a flood of patients every day at the beginning. It will take a while for people to get used to having a doctor right in town."

"I'm already used to it," Caroline said, laughing. "I'm so glad you took the job!" They discussed details and settled on the next Monday to begin the course. "You can check on Lena while you're here," she added. "That will be convenient."

Not necessarily, Rachel thought. She preferred the

structure of an office visit for seeing her patients. It helped her maintain detachment. "I'll be sure to set her up for regular appointments when the clinic opens."

"Perfect," Caroline said. "Thanks so much. And we will expect you Monday for first aid, if not before."

Rachel hung up the phone and then sat with her head in her hand, her eyes closed. Instead of staying out of Garrett's way, she was now going to be seeing him on a daily basis, going to his home to teach first aid to his camp kids. It would have been bad enough to deal with him when Lena came to the office, but in that kind of professional setting Rachel was certain she could keep control.

On his territory, she wasn't so sure the same would be true. The situation would be much less predictable. He would forget to keep his distance, and he'd smile. Or even flirt with her, as he was so skilled at doing. And with her attention distracted, how often would she respond in kind? This plan of Caroline's was a personal disaster, as far as Rachel was concerned.

But she had agreed, so she would simply have to deal with the situation. Maybe Garrett wouldn't attend the first-aid sessions—he might have ranch work to do. That would be the best-case scenario. If he did attend, she'd simply be polite but cool. Focus on the kids and what they were learning, not the handsome minister in the cowboy hat. She'd often seen patients all day after going without sleep the night before, so she could handle this kind of stress, too.

She would have to. Getting too close to Garrett Marshall posed not only a personal risk, she had come to realize, but a professional one, as well. To make a success of her medical practice, she had to be viewed as an authority figure—a knowledgeable and reliable physician.

Her patients would include ranchers and laborers working in the area, some of them men like Lena's father who didn't easily accept the competence of a young woman. Being the local pastor's girlfriend could weaken her in their eyes and diminish their confidence in her skills. An old codger in Idaho had once dismissed her as "that cute little girl."

So she would keep Garrett at arm's length as she established her practice. Maybe in the future, when the locals trusted her, there would be an opportunity for a romantic relationship. Garrett wouldn't wait, of course—he would find a woman with similar beliefs to be his wife and give him those kids he wanted.

That surprisingly disturbing concept kept her awake far longer than she would have preferred.

Chapter Four

Two days later, Lena was doing well enough with her injections that Dr. Stevens said she could return to the ranch on Thursday. Garrett expected a joyful reaction to that bit of news.

But when he and Justino arrived at the hospital on Thursday morning, Lena was quite subdued. She sat in the chair in her room, appearing younger than her fourteen years.

"We brought your backpack," Justino told her, "to carry your equipment."

"Thanks." She gave him an uncertain smile. "I hope it all fits in there." Boxes of needles took up most of the space in the bag, along with her supply of insulin, an injection log Kim Kaiser had provided, and the books and papers Lena had been reading. The top zipper wouldn't close.

"But you got everything in there," Garrett said, trying for the positive perspective. "We'll figure out how to store this stuff when we get to the Circle M. Maybe a plastic box of some kind. For now, though, are you ready to go?"

Lena glanced around reluctantly, as if the room had been somewhere she'd enjoyed staying and didn't want to leave. "I guess so."

Once outside, she stopped and took a deep breath. "It's

nice to be in the fresh air." Lifting her face to the sun, she grinned. "I was tired of that hospital smell."

"I'm not surprised." Garrett unlocked the truck and watched as the teenagers climbed into the backseat. "Let's make a plan not to come here again."

Lena giggled. "Okay."

Justino spoke as Garrett accelerated onto the interstate. "I'm so glad you're coming back, Lena. I've missed you so much."

"Me, too."

Through the rearview mirror, Garrett saw Lena put her head on the boy's shoulder, but after only a moment, she sat up again. "Mr. Garrett, am I going to have to eat different food from everybody else?"

"I've talked with Caroline and Susannah about the meals," he told her. "We're going to make a few changes that the others won't mind—less pasta and bread, more vegetables and proteins. It'll be healthier for everybody. And then you can make good choices."

"What about dessert?"

"Well, there you're going to have to be strong. We can't quit making dessert altogether, but we can have fruits available so you can don't have to go without something sweet."

"But I love ice cream."

"Me, too. And homemade is the best, isn't it?" Garrett had considered this problem all week long. "But I'll give up ice cream if you will."

She met his gaze in the mirror. "Why would you do that?"

He shrugged a shoulder. "Maybe it won't be so hard if you aren't suffering alone. Besides, I could stand to drop a few pounds. I've been eating too well these past few weeks."

"You're making that up."

"Nope. Deal?"

After a long pause, Lena said, "Deal."

As he said a silent farewell to his favorite dessert, she came up with another question. "Will Dr. Vale be there when we get to the ranch?"

I wish. "We didn't ask her to be there. Is something wrong?"

"No, I just wondered if maybe she wanted to make sure I was doing things right when I got out of the hospital."

"I didn't think about that." He gave himself a mental punch. "We can call her when we get to the house." The first of what would no doubt be many calls for Rachel's attention.

Not on his account, of course. When he'd encountered her at the hospital this week he had struggled to stay casual, to act uninterested. And it *was* an act—each time he saw her, he liked her more, was more stirred by her presence. Hiding his emotions proved a difficult task. Her concern for Lena and her attention to the girl's condition demonstrated what a vital resource Rachel would be for the people of his little town.

"That's okay," Lena said. "I don't want to bother her. I can handle it." Doubt colored her tone.

Garrett dredged up more reassurance. "I'm sure you can. And I've been reading up. I can go over your dosage with you before you inject."

"Right." It was not a vote of confidence.

He didn't have Rachel's number in his cell phone, or he would have called at that moment. Whether she wanted a relationship with him or not, Lena's situation was of primary concern. He could behave himself for her sake.

The three people in the truck gave a mutual sigh of

relief when he turned in to the drive for the Circle M. In just a few minutes the house and the barn came into sight. Lena sat forward, staring through the windshield.

"I'm glad to be here," she told Garrett. "I missed it."

"And I'm glad to hear that," he said with a grin. "We must be doing something right."

When they pulled to a stop at the house, the only resident visible was Honey, the golden retriever, lying stretched out in a patch of sunshine on the front porch. As Garrett put the truck in park, the dog stood up and came down the steps to greet them.

Lena nearly fell out of the vehicle in her rush to hug the dog. "Honey! I'm so happy to see you!" She laughed as Honey licked her face. "Yes, I love you, too." Glancing around, she seemed disappointed. "Where is everybody?"

Garrett suspected he'd heard a shushing noise come through the screen door from the direction of the living room.

"I'm not sure," he said, suppressing a grin. "Maybe we should check the house?"

"They might be out riding," Justino said. His dark eyes were smiling—he'd heard the whispers from inside, too.

"Humph." Lena got to her feet and walked to the door, opened it…and squealed. "No!"

"Surprise!" the kids inside yelled at the tops of their voices. "Welcome back!"

When Garrett got to the doorway, he saw a banner hung across the wall with the same message painted on it. Balloons floated near the ceiling and streamers littered the floor. Lena sat on the couch with Lizzie and Becky on either side of her, the three of them chattering simultaneously. The three boys—Nate, Thomas and Marcos—lounged nearby, trying to look bored and failing.

Ford and Caroline stood to the side, grinning at the

successful celebration. "Good job," Garrett said, joining them. "She had no idea."

"It was Lizzie's suggestion." Caroline was obviously satisfied with her campers' effort. "But the boys didn't protest. I consider that a big win."

"And we didn't even have to bribe them with food," Ford added.

"That's a surprise." Garrett heard Honey's bark outside. "Are we expecting visitors?"

"Yes, as a matter of fact." Caroline went to open the screen door. "Hi, Rachel, come in. How are you?"

This surprise stole Garrett's breath for a few seconds. He couldn't help drinking in the sight of her—the russet hair pulled to the side and then into a ponytail, the smooth cream of her cheeks and the shining blue of her eyes. Khaki shorts showed off the toned length of her legs and a sleeveless yellow shirt revealed her slender arms. His mouth went dry even as he fought to school his face into a casual—damn the word—mask.

When she turned toward him, he didn't offer his hand for her to shake. "Hey, Rachel. What brings you out this way?"

"I called her," Caroline said. "I wondered if maybe Lena would appreciate having Rachel around for her solo flight, so to speak."

"You're one smart woman. Lena was actually hoping Rachel would be here." He met the doctor's gaze, keeping his own cool. "Thanks for making a house call."

"I'm glad to help." She nodded toward the welcome banner. "This appears to be a party."

"A surprise party," he agreed. "Lena was pretty thrilled."

"That's great for her confidence. She must have been a little nervous returning to her friends."

"Try a lot nervous. But so far, all is well."

"We planned to have lunch down at the creek," Caroline said. "Can you stay, Rachel? We'd love to have you."

"Sure," she said, after a moment's hesitation. "Sounds like fun."

Garrett didn't believe he imagined the wariness that flashed through the doctor's blue eyes. If Rachel were as immune to him as she claimed, why would she be reluctant to stay?

Susannah Bradley, who had recently taken over as housekeeper and cook, brought two picnic baskets into the living room. "Who's toting lunch today?"

Her son, Nate, volunteered, as he usually did, but the other boys didn't offer to help. "I can carry a basket," Lena said. "It's not heavy."

Garrett opened his mouth to protest, but then had second thoughts. He snagged Rachel's attention. "She has to test her blood sugar and take an injection before doing anything else, especially eating."

Rachel nodded. "That's right."

"But she's not showing any sign that she remembers. Do I remind her, in front of her friends? Do I let her get all the way to the creek and have to leave again to take care of her medical needs? How am I supposed to handle this?"

The kids were preparing to exit the house and start the walk down to the creek running through the Circle M land. Lena had left her backpack sitting on the floor by the couch and picked up one of the picnic baskets. Justino stood beside her, offering to help her carry the load.

"This is the kind of dilemma you'll be coming up against. I think you have to remind her," Rachel said, finally. "Either she's pretending it doesn't matter or she actually forgot. And Justino isn't helping. But she can't ignore what must be done."

"Right." Taking a deep breath, Garrett crossed to the door just as Lena and Justino started to leave. "Hold up, Lena."

She stared up at him, and the light went out of her face. "Oh, yeah."

"Yeah. You've got something to do."

"Couldn't I do it after lunch? I'm hungry."

"I'm glad you're hungry. But you know that's not how it works."

She sighed. "Justino, you take the basket. I'll be there in a while."

"Sure." His cheeks flushed, and he gave Garrett a guilty glance. "Sorry."

Rachel joined them. "Would you like me to go with you?" she asked Lena. "I can double-check your dose."

"Maybe," Lena said. "Just this first time. To be sure."

"Lead the way," Rachel said, following the girl through the door. On the threshold, though, she looked back into the house and gave Garrett a thumbs-up sign, plus a smile and a wink.

Ford had come to stand beside him. "That was tricky."

Garrett shook his head. "This parenting stuff is not for sissies."

"You and the doctor make a great team."

"She's another smart lady."

"Don't sell yourself short, brother. You're the one who called Lena to account, and you did it without causing a scene for her or for you. Well done."

"Thanks." As always, his brother's praise felt good.

But it was a wink and a smile from the pretty redhead that put the big grin on his face.

RACHEL FOLLOWED LENA up the hill to a small timber-sided house with a wide front porch.

"This is where the girls stay," Lena said, leading the way up the front steps. "The boys are in the bunkhouse."

"Just like the ranch hands in the old days, hmm?"

"I guess so." Inside the house, Lena looked around. "Where am I supposed to do this? In the bathroom? The kitchen? The bedroom?"

"Wherever you're comfortable." Even though she'd treated diabetics in the past, Rachel had never contemplated all the small details that would go into daily life. "You would have the most privacy in the bathroom, I suppose."

"But it's not very big. Maybe I'll just use the kitchen for now. We're not cooking in here."

"Do you have your orders from the doctor?"

Lena put her backpack on the counter and began pulling out materials. "They're in there somewhere." When she finished, a jumble of papers, books and boxes had been spread over the workspace. "Let me find them."

Rachel waited, and cautioned herself not to say anything about being more organized. She wasn't the parent, and Lena would have to develop her own system. But staying quiet was a struggle.

"Here it is." Lena handed the sheets to Rachel. "First I have to test."

"Are you sure?"

"What else—oh." The girl nodded. "First, wash your hands."

"Right."

From there the process continued in a haphazard fashion. "Where's the glucose meter?" Another search revealed the meter kit. "Put the strip in the meter. Put the lancet in the gun." She glanced at Rachel with a frown.

"That's what I call it because it seems like you're shooting yourself with that little needle."

Teenagers had some unique perspectives. "There is a resemblance."

"Then pick a finger and click." A wince greeted the prick of the lancet. "Now catch blood on the strip and wait for the number." Five seconds ticked by in silence. "Huh. It's high. I barely ate any breakfast."

"Don't blame yourself," Rachel said. "Just write it down and figure out your insulin dose. You'll be eating bread at lunch, so you want to take that into consideration."

"This is such a pain." Brow furrowed, Lena studied the instruction sheet and her log book then came up with a number. "Do I have it right?"

Rachel scanned her work. "You've got it. Do you want me to give you the injection? Or step out and give you privacy?"

"Could you just make sure I'm holding the syringe right? How am I supposed to tell what a forty-five-degree angle looks like?" She picked up the insulin pen, dialed up a dose and then drew a deep breath. "Now for the bad part."

Lifting her shirt, Lena pinched a fold of skin on her stomach, below her waist. "Like this?" she asked, posing the needle.

"That's it," Rachel told her. "Go for it."

With a breath hissing between her teeth, Lena pushed the needle into the fold of skin. Her thumb fumbled for the button at the end of the pen, then pushed.

"'Remember to pause at the bottom,'" she parodied Kim in a high-pitched voice, "'so the last drop leaves the needle.'" She frowned. "It still hurts. Every single time."

"You will get used to it, honey." She couldn't help

feeling sympathetic. "You've been doing this less than a week."

"Seems like forever already. Can we go to lunch now? I'm starved."

At this point, silence wasn't an option. "Aren't you forgetting something?"

"What?"

A raised eyebrow and a glance at the mess was Rachel's answer.

Lena sighed. "I have to clean up, I suppose." She rushed through the process, stuffing supplies into the backpack without order while Rachel again bit her tongue. Step by step, they would get through this.

Finally, the girl shoved her pack into the corner of the countertop. "Now can we go?"

"Sure. Congratulations on your first solo injection."

"Not really solo," Lena said as they crossed the porch. "You were here."

"But you handled it correctly. I just watched."

"Will you be here for dinner? Can you help me again?"

Rachel hesitated. She'd already stepped beyond her usual boundaries. But Lena obviously required the support. "I'll be here at dinner."

"Great! This way to the creek."

They crested the hill beside the big red barn and then started down the other side. Where the slope flattened out, a wooden bridge crossed the rocky stream curving along the edge of the fields beyond. On the near side, a couple of picnic tables sat under the shade of cottonwood trees, with teenagers gathered around, filling their plates. Lena ran to join them as Rachel walked over to the adults standing close by.

"Everything went just fine," she said in answer to Garrett's questioning expression. "Lena got the dose right and injected herself."

He blew out a breath and grinned. "That's a relief. Thanks for being here."

She cautioned herself not to soften in response to his concern. "I'm glad to help her set up her routine."

"And now you deserve some lunch as a reward," he said, holding out a hand toward the tables. "Let me introduce you to Susannah Bradley, the chef of today's feast. And that's her daughter, Amber, peeking out from behind her."

Rachel shook hands with the pretty blonde woman. "It's quite a task, pleasing teenagers' appetites." She sent a smile to the little girl, who promptly withdrew, out of sight.

"I enjoy the challenge," Susannah said. "My son, Nate, lets me know when I get it right." She nodded toward one of the boys sitting by the creek. "At five years old, Amber's not so picky. I hope you enjoy your lunch, too."

"If the kids have left any food for us," Garrett said. "They're a ravenous bunch."

"That's the nature of the beast," Ford said. "Teenagers are always hungry."

"Especially when you keep them busy." Caroline handed Rachel a bottle of water. "Which is what we try to do. We don't usually have leftovers these days."

"Reminds me of when you two were growing up." Wyatt nodded toward his brothers. "You licked the plates so clean, you barely had to wash them after dinner."

Caroline rolled her eyes. "Spoken like a true guy."

Rachel laughed. "Definitely."

"Dylan was the hungriest," Garrett protested. "We could never fill him up. Still can't."

A dark-haired newcomer stepped up to join them, a

Marshall brother by the look of him. "Still can't what?" he asked.

"Just talking about your famous appetite," Garrett told him. "Rachel, this is our youngest brother. Dylan, meet Rachel Vale, the new doctor in town."

"Hello, there." Dylan offered a handshake and a sexy smile. "I'm glad to meet you. I'll have that big sign of yours finished up in a few days."

"Terrific. Thanks for doing that." Each of the brothers had a different appearance, yet the strong, handsome faces showed an undeniable resemblance. Seen all together, they were quite a striking group.

And if she considered Garrett the most attractive of the four, well, what difference did that make anyway?

The kids had taken their plates and found places to sit on the rocks edging the creek bed. Rachel located a boulder of her own and settled down to eat. She wasn't sure whether to be relieved or piqued when Garrett chose a spot away some distance, near Susannah Bradley and Amber. Judging by his laughter, he enjoyed their company quite a lot. Not that Rachel was listening.

"So what do you think of Bisons Creek so far?" Dylan sat down beside her with a plate full of sandwiches. "Not quite Seattle, is it?"

"That's not a bad thing," Rachel said. "I enjoy the sunshine every day, rather than clouds and drizzle. And it's a beautiful landscape. I love the rolling plains, the mountains and the wide sky above them."

"Yeah, it's a pretty special part of the country. I went away for a few years, but I don't plan to leave again."

"Garrett said you're a sculptor. That must be a challenge to combine with ranch work."

"It has been, especially this summer. We've hired a new cowboy recently, though, and he's taken some of the load off. He would have been at lunch, but he's out checking fence line today. We're all doing two jobs—Ford's got a law practice in town, Caroline still has her work with the Family Services office, and Garrett's supposed to preach a sermon this weekend. I wonder if he's written it yet."

"Is it strange, listening to your brother speak from the pulpit?"

"Not really—he's always telling me what to do." Dylan laughed as he got to his feet. "Being a minister was all he ever wanted, almost as far back as I can remember. No matter what else was going on—rodeo shows, calving, storms or blizzards, Garrett was always at church on Sunday morning." He took her empty plate and headed toward the trash bag tied to a tree.

Rachel let her gaze wander to the man in question, now talking with Ford and Caroline. Before she could look away, he caught her watching. He didn't smile.

Dylan's recollection confirmed some of her reasons for keeping Garrett at a distance. His commitment to his calling and the church he served couldn't be ignored. However strong her attraction to him might be, the clash between their points of view would only produce pain.

As if to test her resolve, he chose that moment to close the distance between them.

"Did you get enough to eat? There are still a few sandwiches left."

"I did, thanks. It was delicious. Susannah must be a wonderful cook." The words cost her some effort to say.

But Garrett was all enthusiasm. "You wouldn't believe the dinners she's been serving up. We're all buying our jeans a size larger these days."

Having noticed his flat waist and slim hips, Rachel didn't believe that one. "Her son is one of the campers?"

"Right. Nate's a born horseman—I'll be surprised if we don't have him hanging around permanently. Which would be okay. He's a good kid."

"And Susannah is your housekeeper? Has she been with you long?" Rachel didn't want to examine her reasons for asking.

"Only a few weeks. Her husband was causing trouble, so Susannah and Amber came out here to be safe. Now we're wondering how we ever managed without her. Wyatt says he's never eaten so well. Given that we've always taken turns cooking, I believe him."

She couldn't help being curious. "I gather the four of you were self-sufficient as you grew up."

"We did pretty well taking care of ourselves, though there were definitely some lean times, especially before Ford got his job after school at the hardware store. But we survived. How about you?" he asked, propping a hip on the boulder next to hers. "What were your teen years about? Besides studying, of course. You must have been smart to get into medical school."

"That was pretty much the story," she said, steering the conversation in a casual direction. "I had a single mom who worked two jobs and couldn't spend much time at home. I kept the house neat and did my homework."

"In Seattle?"

"Actually, I grew up in a little town about an hour north of Laramie."

"A Wyoming woman, born and raised? Is that why you came here to practice?"

"That, and my scholarship required me to work here after training. But it's no hardship. The rain in Seattle was a hardship."

"It would be for me, too. Did you always want to be a doctor?"

Not an impersonal question, but she could deflect it. "Pretty much. That was the goal for smart kids at school." He didn't need more details.

But of course he asked for them. "I suspect you had more than academic ambition as a motive. Most physicians I've talked to do."

Now she had to choose between being viewed as a snob and sharing some very personal information. "My mother had high blood pressure and a chronic kidney condition. We visited many doctors over the years who tried to help her manage her illness. I always thought they seemed to be in control of their lives." She had to smile at her own delusion. "Now I know that's not always the case. My mother would follow their directions and do better for a while, then fall away from her eating plan and prescriptions and get worse. As a teenager, I wanted to be the person in control, helping patients improve and then stay well."

Garrett nodded. "My mom had a chronic lung disease that eventually killed her. That kind of experience shapes you in ways you don't always realize when you're a kid." He gave her a wink. "See, we do have something in common."

She wouldn't concede that point so she tried deflecting again. "You and your family are giving these kids a chance to be shaped by the positive memory of your concern and attention this summer. That's a very special kind of influence."

"We hope so. I hear you're going to be part of the program next week, teaching lessons in first aid."

The change of subject was a relief. "That's the plan. I've ordered them each a manual that they'll be able to keep."

"What a great idea! I'm not sure all of them will use it, but some definitely will."

"You do have an interesting mix of personalities." She was watching two of the boys wrestling in the creek, grappling with each other while striving to keep their footing on the rocks under the water.

Garrett followed her line of sight. "That's Thomas Gray Cloud, the shorter one, and Marcos Oxendine. Our toughest customers, so to speak. They're always sparring with each other, with words if not fists."

"They've come to blows?"

"Oh, yes. Both of them have hair-trigger tempers."

Even as he said the words, the pretend wrestling became earnest. After taking a punch that should have been light but clearly wasn't, Thomas snarled and lunged at Marcos, grabbing him around the shoulders and bearing him backward. The other boy shouted and tried to push him off, then resorted to pulling his opponent's hair.

Ford and Dylan headed for the fight, with Garrett close behind. Before they could reach the pair, Marcos lost his balance on the uneven creek bed and fell backward, with Thomas on top of him.

One of the girls screamed.

The rest of the crowd watched in horror as Marcos's head banged against a sharp-edged stone.

Chapter Five

Ford and Dylan pulled Thomas away. Garrett bent over Marcos. "You okay, son?" Gripping the boy's shoulders, he looked into his face. "Still with us?"

Wincing, Marcos raised a hand to the back of his head. "That hurt." His expression froze suddenly, and he brought his hand in front of him. "I'm bleeding," he said in a shaky voice. "My head is bleeding."

"Does your neck hurt?" Rachel stood at Garrett's elbow with a thick pad of napkins in her hand.

Marcos stared at her in confusion. "No. Why should it?"

"Do you know what day it is?"

"Thursday."

"Where are you?"

"In the creek where that stupid *pendejo* pushed me."

One side of her mouth quirked in a smile. "Where is the creek?"

He looked at her in annoyance. "The ranch. The Circle M Ranch. Why are you asking me dumb questions?"

Garrett scowled at him. "To make sure you're okay. Be polite."

Marcos rolled his eyes. "Can I get out of the water? I'm all wet."

Rachel watched his face, her gaze intent. She had her fingers at his wrist, taking a pulse. "Are you dizzy?"

"No."

"Sick to your stomach?"

"No. Just wet. And bleeding."

"Hold this on the cut." Rachel slipped the napkins behind his head and put his hand over them. "Even small head wounds bleed a lot," she told him, her voice calm. Then she glanced at Garrett. "Let's help him up."

Once on his feet, Marcos straightened his shoulders. "I'm okay. No big deal." The boy was getting his bravado back.

"I'm the doctor," Rachel said. "I get to decide what's a big deal." She looked at Garrett. "Where's the first-aid kit?"

"At the house." Ford had already marched Thomas toward the barn, no doubt with some sort of penalty chore in mind.

"We'll walk with him to be sure he doesn't faint."

"I ain't gonna faint," Marcos declared. But his face was pale.

"Why do the two of you go after each other?" Garrett asked as they headed up the hill, with Rachel on one side of the kid and himself on the other. "Can't you just leave him alone?"

"He can just leave *me* alone." Marcos checked the bloody napkin, grimaced and put it back on his head. "He started it."

"You hit him hard."

"I was kidding around."

"You know what a temper he has."

"I got my own temper. And I don't take stuff off little runts like him."

"So now you're after revenge." Garrett grimaced at Rachel, who frowned.

Marcos shrugged his free shoulder. "If the chance comes around…"

"Have you ever heard of turning the other cheek?"

"What?"

"Letting an insult go. Not getting revenge."

"What kind of man does that?"

"One who wants peace."

The boy shook his head. "Crazy. You'd lose all your status."

"But you wouldn't keep getting hurt, or hurting others. This kind of violence will get you into serious trouble."

They reached the front porch and opened the screen door. Marcos walked in before Rachel, but Garrett motioned her ahead of him.

"First-aid kit?" she asked. "And a room with bright light?"

"The kitchen." Garrett led the way and pulled out a chair for Marcos at the table. Then he fetched the emergency box from its cabinet. "Here you go."

"Nice and big," Rachel commented, pulling on gloves. "You've got everything I could ask for, since I doubt stitches are required. Put your head on your arms, Marcos. Let me examine this cut."

The bleeding had stopped and, after cleaning the cut, she confirmed stitches weren't necessary. Fifteen minutes later, with a bandage wrapped around his head, Marcos resembled a wounded warrior. "Thanks," he said, without meeting Rachel's eyes. "Can I go now?"

"You can go to the bunkhouse to change," Garrett said. "And spend the afternoon without television or games on your phone. Read a book if you want something to do."

Muttering, Marcos left the house, letting the screen door bang loudly on his way out.

"I don't know how to get through to him...or to Thomas." Garrett threw the bandage wrappers in the trash. "Talking hasn't made a dent so far. Extra chores and curtailed privileges don't work, either. I have to wonder if we're bound for failure with those two."

Rachel raised a skeptical eyebrow. "And I thought you were an optimist. Aren't ministers supposed to find the good in people?"

"I do find good in those boys. They're strong and confident and determined. With the right goals, they could both build successful lives." He shook his head. "But how do I get them to understand that violence doesn't solve problems?"

"They might take more than a few weeks to learn that lesson." She closed the first-aid box. "You and your brothers are doing what's most important—giving them examples of four honest, patient, hardworking men who solve their problems with their brains, not their fists. Just by being who you are, you're demonstrating what Thomas and Marcos can become."

He held her gaze. "That's the nicest thing you've ever said to me."

She looked away then, her cheeks flushing. "It's just what I've observed."

"Thanks for the vote of confidence. For what it's worth, I think you're pretty special, too."

Her defenses sprang up. "You shouldn't say that."

"Of course I should. It's true."

"We agreed to keep things casual."

"I'm really starting to hate that word." He tried to rein in his frustration. "Ignoring what's between us won't make it disappear."

Her blue gaze turned fierce. "Yes, it will."

Around them, the house was still and quiet. Garrett knew they were completely alone. Reaching out, he took Rachel's hands in his. "So you're just going to pretend you don't feel anything when my fingers touch yours." He linked their fingers and pressed their palms together.

"That's right." But she swallowed hard.

"And it wouldn't make any difference if I stroked your hair." He let go of her left hand and skimmed his fingers lightly over the smooth strands above her ear.

"No." Her fingers twitched in his grasp.

"So a simple kiss wouldn't matter at all."

She drew a deep breath. "Of course not."

"Okay, then." He leaned forward and set his lips against hers.

Rachel didn't pull away—he suspected she might be testing herself. He kissed her gently, exploring the sweet shape of her mouth, the smoothness of the soft flesh. She gasped, and her lips parted slightly, giving him more room to play, to coax, to invite.

Her lips moved against his, tentatively, reluctantly.

"No obligation," he whispered. "No strings attached."

She relaxed under his touch, and started to return the kiss. The sensation went straight through him, head to toe, and his pulse jumped in his veins. But he kept himself in control, letting Rachel set the speed now. He didn't want to scare her away.

But she was the one who took the contact deeper, who stepped closer so that their bodies touched. Her hand came to his shoulder, holding tight as their kisses veered toward wild. Mouths sliding and clinging, the nip of teeth and the graze of a tongue—Garrett's restraint was slipping. He ached to use his hands, to explore the curve of her hip and the swell of her breast. This was as close to lust as he'd come in a long, long time.

And so, between one kiss and the next, he lifted his head. "Not so simple, after all," he said, his voice unsteady. "Maybe you can ignore this. I can't."

Rachel dropped her chin, which left her forehead resting against his chest. "You've made it very hard."

"Or it could be very easy to just explore where this goes, what we could find together."

She sighed, lifted her head and stepped back. Their fingers slowly untwined. "I don't believe that, for the reasons I've already given you. There's no point in building a relationship that's going to fail." Her somber blue gaze met his. "I also think a romance between us would make it harder for me to do my job with some patients. I can't afford that."

Now that was an unanswerable argument. "I wouldn't want to hurt your career."

She gave him a small smile. "I'm glad you understand." Turning, she walked to the kitchen door before looking over her shoulder. "Tell Lena I'll come back to see her at dinnertime." Her footsteps echoed through the empty house and across the front porch. In the quiet, he could hear her SUV start and head down the drive.

Garrett let his head hang and rubbed his hands over his face. His body still hummed with the desire incited by Rachel's kisses…heart-stealing kisses he would never regret having tasted.

But now she'd decided a connection between them would interfere with her practice. In that case, what could he do but leave her alone?

Out in the living room, the screen door slapped against the frame. Boot heels sounded on the hardwood floors—

Wyatt's by the sound of the steps. Garrett sat on a stool at the kitchen counter as his brother came into the kitchen.

"Did you get the boy patched up?" Setting his hat on the table, he started to make a cup of coffee. "Will he be okay?"

"Just a cut and a bruise," Garrett said. "Rachel put a bandage on it and I sent him to the bunkhouse to consider his sins."

Wyatt snorted. "I'm sure that will happen. Those two kids are a combustible combination." He joined Garrett at the counter. "Where is Rachel? I figured she might stay the afternoon."

"She…uh…had to leave, but she'll be here to check in with Lena before dinner."

"Bisons Creek has got itself a real attractive doctor to visit." Wyatt chuckled. "All the ranchers in the county will be going in for checkups."

Garrett didn't find the idea funny. "I guess so."

His big brother shot him a shrewd glance. "And you'll be one of them."

He shook his head. "What I want from Rachel Vale is not a medical exam."

"Sounds like there's a problem with what you want."

"She won't date a minister."

"Why the hell not?"

"She's got some problems with my approach to life."

"Then maybe you're better off without her."

"She also said being involved with me would be bad for her career."

Wyatt thought for a minute. "There are a few old guys around here who might give her a hard time about it. But then, they'll probably give her a hard time just because she's a woman."

"Right." Garrett drew a deep breath. "But I can't get

her off my mind. When you find somebody who just fits, it's damn hard to give up the possibility, you know?"

"Yeah." They sat in silence for a while, until Wyatt stirred. "All you can do is be patient. If it's meant to be, she'll change her mind."

"Not if we never actually communicate."

"She's gonna be here every day next week. If you can't manage to make some headway with her while she's on the place, then you're not working hard enough."

"Good point, brother," Garrett said, regaining some of his confidence. "Good point."

THURSDAY NIGHT, RACHEL decided she had to talk to someone. And at this particular moment, when her brain had become oatmeal and common sense had completely deserted her, there was only one person to call.

"Hi, Dee. Are you busy?"

"Hey, Rache!" Deirdre Ames, her best friend in Seattle, clicked her tongue. "I'm never busy where you're concerned. How are you? How was the drive to Back of Beyond, Wyoming?"

"No problem. I arrived Monday morning as planned. Sorry I haven't called, but an emergency came up before I'd been here an hour and I spent a lot of the week with that patient."

"Nothing like jumping in at the deep end. Everything all right?"

"A teenager on the edge of ketoacidosis, now diagnosed with diabetes. You understand how hard that adjustment can be."

"Tough one." Dee was a pediatrician with plenty of experience in juvenile diabetes. "Hope her parents are up to speed."

"Not exactly. Her mother is dead and her father refuses to cooperate. I'm kind of helping Lena get used to managing her condition on her own."

"You can't do that forever."

"No, but we're figuring things out as we go."

"Not your normal style—you usually make plans way ahead. And who is we?"

"The other adult in this scenario is Garrett Marshall. He's in charge of the camp Lena's attending at his ranch. He's made himself responsible for her and I'm supposed to be his medical support." She couldn't repress a sigh at the thought.

And her friend heard it. "Why is that a problem? Is he a pain in the butt?"

"Oh, no. He's a really nice guy."

"That's promising. Handsome?"

"Definitely."

"Where's the difficulty? Sounds like a perfect setup."

Rachel took a deep breath. "He's a minister."

"Oh." Dee was silent for a long moment. "That's too bad. Well, you just meet with him for Lena's appointments and let it go. Right?"

"He's...interested in more." Rachel revisited this afternoon in the kitchen. "He kissed me."

"Is he a good kisser?"

"Incredible."

"*Incredible?* I've never heard you say that about a guy before."

"Garrett is different than anybody I've met before."

After a pause, Dee cleared her throat. "Have you explained to him about your mom?"

"Only that she died. I'm trying to keep things casual between us." She remembered what he'd said about hating that word. "Not sharing too much."

"You kissed him!"

"He kissed me first. I thought I could keep it in control."

"You always think that. Maybe for once you ought to let go and just follow where it leads."

"It leads straight to disaster. He's honest and reliable, as well as charming, but—"

"That makes him totally different from those guys who took advantage of your mom. They were criminals, Rache, not well-meaning pastors. Are you really attracted to him?"

Rachel sighed. "More attracted than I've ever been to anyone else."

"So maybe…just maybe…you could give this guy a chance."

"What would be the point? I'm also worried that I'll lose the respect of my patients if I'm known as the local preacher's girlfriend."

"I can't say that wouldn't happen." Deirdre took an audible breath. "Still, you shouldn't have to live like a nun just because you're a doctor."

"But his faith and his church are part of who he is. How can I be so drawn to him when I can't share that aspect of his life?"

Her friend laughed. "You don't want to hear my answer to that question."

"Give it to me."

"You won't believe it."

"I'll listen."

"No, you won't. You'll put up defenses against whatever's happening here. I'm not going to help you do that."

"Deirdre!"

"Call me back when you figure it out. I'll be waiting." She ended the call.

Rachel barely stopped herself from throwing her

phone across the room. Dee could be a soft shoulder to cry on, but she could also be the most frustrating person on the planet when she decided to help you for your own good.

Of course she needed defenses against Garrett Marshall. What had happened when she left herself vulnerable? Those kisses in the kitchen, that's what, which would be hard for her to forget. The strength of his shoulder under her hand, the scent of lime from his skin, the shape of his mouth and the way it fit so perfectly over hers…

…were not things she should dwell on. And, for Rachel, the antidote to ruminating was always action.

Two hours later, having vacuumed the whole apartment, cleaned the bathroom and swept the front porch, she'd finally worked off enough frustration to get ready for bed.

But with the light off and the quiet Wyoming night outside her open window, her mind homed in on Garrett and the predicament he presented.

The problem was, she did want more than casual with Garrett Marshall. She'd been struck that first day by his care for Lena, his willingness to take on the girl's situation and deal with it rather than handing it off to someone else. Responsible and committed, he cared for others before himself, a quality that appealed to her as a woman and as a doctor. He did it with a sense of humor, too, which worked well when it came to handling prickly teenagers. Not to mention defensive physicians.

But what her heart wanted and what her head insisted was smart—safe—were entirely different. Garrett threatened her equanimity in a way she'd never experienced before. He tempted her to give in to her feelings, which were all in his favor.

In her experience, though, letting emotions guide you

led to a life like her mother's—volatile and uncontrolled. Rachel had never been sure, growing up, what would happen next in her world. One day, her mother's health would be good, the next she'd require a trip to the emergency room. Sometimes bills would be paid, others the electricity would be disconnected. The new boyfriend might be the man of her mother's dreams. Or another jerk. And all of it depending on her mother's *feelings*.

In the end, attempting a relationship with Garrett was simply too big a risk. She was starting a new medical practice, a new *life*, and she couldn't afford to let sentiment get in the way. The best plan would be to keep things simple between them. Just friendship. Just *casual*. That way, neither of them would get hurt and her life would continue to be what she wanted. Practical. Logical. Self-sufficient.

If solitary.

TRUE TO HER WORD, Rachel returned the evening of Lena's homecoming to supervise the girl's dinnertime injection. But she dashed off again with just a few words to Caroline, so Garrett didn't have a chance to talk with her. He was pretty disgruntled about that.

Supervising dinner preparations took most of his attention, however. Thomas and Marcos were on the same team and, after this afternoon's fight, were not inclined to cooperate with each other or anyone else. Their attitudes made getting hamburgers grilled an exercise in patience. Luckily Becky and Justino were there to manage the details and ensure a complete meal was served.

All the kids loved having burgers, but Garrett noticed that Lena was especially enthusiastic.

"This looks *so* good," she said, adding baked beans to her plate. "I'm starved." She skipped over the big bowl of green salad and went for the potato chips. "Yum." She took one off her plate and popped it into her mouth.

Garrett stepped up beside her. "Salad would be a better choice for crunchy."

She pouted. "I'll get some later. My plate is full."

"You'll be full if you eat all of that. Maybe throw some of the chips away?"

"I don't want to." Her voice approached a whine. "I've been waiting all day for these. I ate salad at lunch. And fruit."

"Those were excellent choices, the kind you should make most of the time."

Lena pounced on his mistake. "Most of the time I will. Tonight, I want chips." She marched away from him to sit at the table. Justino, who had been behind her in line, avoided Garrett's gaze as he followed.

"How is it possible," Garrett asked Caroline later, "to have an argument about potato chips?"

"You can argue with a teenager about anything," she said. "And a teenager with diabetes might be even more sensitive. You've got a real challenge on your hands. Are you okay with that?"

They were sitting on the edge of the front porch, watching the kids play badminton after dinner. "What choice do I have? Somebody has to be responsible for helping Lena adjust." He shrugged. "And whether I'm ready or not, her dad handed the job to me. I wish Rachel had been here tonight, though. She might have been more persuasive."

"I did invite her to stay, but she said she was expecting a phone call."

Avoiding me is more likely. Garrett's ego still smarted from the idea that a relationship between them would harm her professionally. "I have to say, I'm surprised that someone so bright would choose to practice in little old Bisons Creek at the start of their career. Why wouldn't she choose a bigger city, with more opportunities?"

"Rachel really missed Wyoming, especially when she was in Seattle." Caroline leaned her folded arms on her knees. "And she always felt strongly about 'underserved communities,' as she puts it. The chance to work in a one-doctor town was just what she wanted when she finished her residency in Seattle. I hope the folks around here appreciate how lucky we are to have her."

"So do I." Caroline's comment struck a spark in his mind. "Maybe there ought to be some kind of party to welcome her to the area, introduce our new doctor to her patients. What do you think?"

Her smile wide, Caroline nodded. "It's a terrific idea. Where would we have it?"

"Somewhere in town—maybe Haley Brewster's place. She's got a big yard and all those porches."

"You're just going to inform Mrs. Brewster she has to throw a party and invite the whole town?"

Garrett grinned. "I'll talk to her at church on Sunday. When I'm finished, she'll believe it was all her own idea."

Meanwhile, though, he was supposed to supervise Lena's final injection of the day. He searched for her at curfew and found her at the barn with Justino, standing as close together as they could manage without actually being in an embrace. They separated slightly as he walked up.

"Time for bed," he announced. "Say good-night."

By the longing gazes they exchanged, they might be parting for six months rather than a few hours.

Sighing, Lena followed Garrett to the girls' cabin. Caroline waited for them inside, and he could hear Lizzie and Becky in the bedroom at the rear of the house. He was definitely out of his usual element, but the point was to support Lena, as he had promised.

"So what's the first step?" he asked her.

"Test kit."

He frowned. "Are you sure?"

"Yes," she snapped, rustling through her papers on the kitchen counter. "I'm sure. It says right here—" She stopped and rolled her eyes. "Wash your hands."

"Right."

"I keep forgetting that."

"You'll get used to remembering. This is only your first day solo."

With Caroline observing, they went through the procedure, starting with the blood test. Lena read the meter when it beeped. "Huh. It's high."

"Remember what you had for dinner," Caroline prompted her. "You ate a brownie for dessert."

Garrett nodded. "Those kinds of foods will send your blood-sugar reading up."

"Okay, okay." She prepared her nightly dosage. "I was bad. So sue me."

He remembered some of the reading he'd done on handling kids with diabetes. "Not bad, Lena. Just not making the safest choices."

Frowning, she dialed the dose on her insulin pen and he checked it against the prescription. "Looks right to me. Show Caroline so she understands what you're doing."

"I love being a show-and-tell project." But she took the pen to Caroline to demonstrate how it worked.

The injection itself obviously hurt, but Lena completed it and breathed a sigh of relief. "There. Can I go to bed now?"

Garrett shared the sense of relief. "Sure. See you tomorrow morning."

She gave him a tired smile. "When I have to do the same thing all over again."

"It will get easier." He set a hand on her shoulder and squeezed gently. "Guaranteed."

Caroline followed him out onto the porch, where they found Ford sitting on the swing, waiting.

"I checked in on the boys and they're all set." He stretched out an arm along the back of the bench as Caroline sat beside him. "Are you heading for bed, Garrett?"

He shook his head. "I've got to work on this week's sermon. It's written, but there's a lot of editing to be done."

"Poor Garrett." Caroline put up her hand to smother a yawn. "You've had a hard week, spending so many hours at the hospital. Maybe it will be easier now that Lena's where we can all help take care of her."

"I'm sure it will be. We still need to have a meeting with Rachel so you, at least, understand the details of the process." No matter how Rachel might feel about him, Garrett was certain she would do the best for her patient. Talented, concerned and committed, Rachel Vale was a woman to be depended upon. He would stake his life on that.

"She mentioned she could come out tomorrow," Caroline said. "Maybe that's when we should sit down together. I'll call her early in the morning."

He nodded. "I'll be there. Ford and Dylan can ride with the kids in the meantime."

"If we're not baling hay, moving cattle or keeping Thomas and Marcos from tearing each other apart," Ford said. "We've got plenty of extra time."

"We'll get it all done," Garrett said, too tired to keep the irritation out of his voice. "A little positivity goes a long way."

"You're the one who's short on sleep."

"I'm not complaining."

"No, you just keep taking on more and more responsibility until something has to give. You can't do it all, Garrett."

He managed to quell his irritation. "Thanks for the concern, brother." He gave Ford a salute off his hat brim. "I'll be okay."

Of course, after getting to bed at 2:00 a.m. on Friday morning, he wasn't quite so optimistic when his alarm rang at five. A cold shower and two cups of strong coffee got him moving, though, and the prospect of seeing Rachel in a couple of hours put a smile on his face when he went to wake up the boys.

With breakfast eaten and cleaned up, he helped the kids saddle up for their ride. As he left the barn, he noticed Rachel's SUV approaching on the drive. Caroline and Rachel were already sitting at the dining room table when he came in.

"Thanks for coming," he said, pulling out the chair across from Rachel. "We checked on Lena last night and this morning—everything went according to orders."

She met his gaze directly, but he thought she might be blushing. "From what I observed yesterday," she said, "Lena understands the procedure and can follow it, though she's not organized about the process."

"How long should we plan to supervise her?" Caroline asked.

Rachel shrugged. "As far as the injections are concerned, you can probably trust her to manage on her own now."

Garrett sat forward. "After less than a week? That seems way too soon to me."

"Lena's a smart girl," Rachel said, "and she understands what's at stake. Like most teenagers, she wants to take control of her own body, her own life."

"I agree." Caroline braced her folded arms on the table. "Granted that you're standing in for her parents, Garrett, but Lena should have privacy for her injections. She's an adolescent girl. More important, we want to teach all the teens independence and responsibility while they're here. What better example than allowing Lena to take charge of her treatment?"

"I'm not sure we can risk her physical well-being for the sake of a principle." He scrubbed a hand across his face. "What if she makes a mistake?"

"She'll experience the consequences," Rachel said. "And learn not to make mistakes. Caroline's right—Lena can handle this."

He shook his head. "I think it's asking too much of her at this point."

"In that case, there's another option." She slid some papers toward him. "I did a little research on the internet last night. There's a camp for kids with diabetes in the mountains near Laramie. They offer trained staff, the right kind of support and peers who face the same issues. I called this morning—they have spaces open and scholarships are available."

Folding her hands on the table, she sent him an encouraging smile. "Why not send Lena there?"

Chapter Six

Garrett flushed as if he'd been slapped in the face. "Send her away?"

"Oh, no," Caroline said. "We can't do that."

Rachel hadn't expected the suggestion to meet with immediate approval, so she had prepared her arguments. "On top of everything else you're trying to do, supporting Lena is a huge burden. This other camp is designed for exactly that purpose. Why not give her the benefit of expert care?"

"Lena is not a burden." Garrett's voice, usually so easygoing, had a hard edge. "I won't abandon her the way her dad did."

"You wouldn't be—"

"She'd believe we were. Anyway, how do you imagine we're going to separate her from Justino?"

"That's a point." This discussion was proving to be every bit as difficult as she'd expected. "But you could talk to her and get her reaction to the idea. You might be surprised."

"She'll believe we want to be rid of her," Caroline said. "Because she's too much trouble."

"If you explained—"

Garrett got to his feet. "I know you're trying to find the optimal solution for everybody, Rachel. I just don't agree this is the right one." He scooted the chair in and then stood, gripping the back. "We've developed a relationship with Lena. She trusts us and has faith in us as caregivers. I don't want to jeopardize that by even hinting she should go somewhere else."

She conceded with a nod. "It was a suggestion, that's all. You might browse those pages I printed out. Maybe the diabetes camp would be a possibility for next summer."

"Sure." He smiled, but it wasn't his usual warm expression. "I appreciate your understanding. Can we still call if we have a problem?"

"Of course. I'll assist you however I can. I want Lena to succeed with her diabetes and in the rest of her life."

"Great." He faced Caroline. "Then I guess we can tell Lena she's on her own with her injections, unless she wants to ask for help. Is that the plan?" His tone was grave, his face as somber as Rachel had ever seen it.

She wanted to reassure him. "She'll be okay, Garrett. Being on her own will make her more careful, not less."

"I hope you're right about that." He took a deep breath and blew it out. "Teenagers don't always measure up to their responsibilities. And the consequences, in this situation, are dire."

"Equanimity," she said, with a smile. "Remember? You're suffering over this more than Lena is. She knows what you expect. Give her a chance to earn your trust."

Shaking his head, he walked toward the doorway. "I can't say I won't worry. But I'll try to keep it to myself. Thanks for your help, Rachel. See you later, Caroline." His boot heels thudded on the wooden floor as he crossed the living room and the front porch.

"That," Caroline said, "was Garrett being mad. He

doesn't lose his temper. He gets very quiet and finds a way to leave."

Rachel relaxed against her chair. "I'm sorry he's upset. It's tough being responsible for a teenager with diabetes. Because of the things you can't do for them as much as anything. Will he get over it?"

Her friend nodded. "He'll work through it on his own. But he takes his responsibilities very seriously, whether it's the ranch, the camp or the church."

"So I gathered." Which only reinforced her intention to ignore the impact of yesterday's kisses. Garrett's intense commitment to others meant that if she was involved with him, she'd inevitably have to be involved with his church and the lives of his parishioners, creating pressures that would surely destroy any relationship they might have.

Setting aside that dreary prospect, she glanced over at her friend. "Shall we go over the basics on diabetes? And then I can explain what Lena should be doing to manage her condition."

Caroline straightened up. "Sure. Will there be a test?"

Rachel laughed. "Just a hundred multiple-choice questions."

"Whew. I was worried for a second there."

After an intense forty minutes, Rachel nodded in satisfaction. "I think you're up to speed with this, at least enough to supervise Lena. And you can always call me if you have a question." She gathered the papers they'd been using and stacked them neatly. "Meanwhile, in your spare time, you're going to marry a cowboy and live happily ever after, is that right?"

Caroline's smile lit up her face. "I am. A cowboy lawyer. And you're going to be the small-town doctor who takes care of all our aches and pains. How are you getting along?"

They chatted about the house they shared, though Caroline hadn't been there all week, about Rachel's office and her plans for her practice, about the town itself and the people in it.

"Just be patient," Caroline said as they walked to Rachel's car. "Some of them are pretty set in their ways. It may take a while for them to get used to a new doctor. Especially a woman doctor. These gnarly old ranchers will have to hear from their neighbors that they can trust you."

Rachel nodded. "I worked in similar communities during my residency. I'm not expecting instant acceptance." And she didn't intend to jeopardize her reputation by indulging in a foolish romance…no matter how tempted she might be. "Fortunately, the cost of living out here is much lower than Seattle. My savings will go farther."

"I'm glad you've come." Caroline gave her a sudden hug. "You will be such a blessing for Bisons Creek. And Bisons Creek will be so good for you."

Drawing away, Rachel raised an eyebrow. "What do you think I need?"

"Family," she said promptly. "Give us a chance, and we'll adopt you the way we've adopted these kids."

Laughing, Rachel climbed into the car. "Is that a Marshall brothers' specialty? Taking in strays?" She started the engine before Caroline could answer. "Have a good day!"

As she drove toward town, she considered Caroline's idea that she *needed* family. She was used to being the caretaker, not the one taken care of. Growing up with just her mom, she'd taken on responsibility at an early age. She recalled microwaving dinner for the two of them when she was in the first grade.

So while she appreciated the Marshalls' generosity and acceptance, she wasn't a candidate for adoption. Her independence and self-reliance had propelled her through college, med school and training. Managing on her own didn't bother her.

Being vulnerable did.

STRIDING AWAY FROM the house, Garrett decided that moving hay would be the best way to work off his anger. A couple of hours spent lifting bales would wear the temper right out of him.

Rachel's suggestion about sending Lena to a different camp really bothered him. He'd believed she understood what they were trying to do this summer and would be supportive. Instead she'd found them lacking. Of course, he wanted to do what was best for all the kids, especially Lena. Ripping her away from the people and place she'd come to depend on did not, in his opinion, qualify.

After he'd moved a hundred bales from the trailer to the barn, he was prepared to accept that Rachel was simply trying to help in a way that seemed best to her. She'd only spent a couple of hours on the ranch with the kids, not long enough to appreciate the connections they'd developed with Garrett and his brothers—especially when Thomas and Marcos had chosen her visit as the occasion for a fight.

More contact was the answer, more opportunities for her to observe them all as they shared their days and nights. The first-aid lessons next week would bring her out to the ranch daily, which would be a start. Maybe he could invite her to come one evening for ice cream or a campfire. She'd encounter the Circle M summer camp at its best. Then, he was sure, she'd understand.

With noon approaching, he caught up with Lena in

the tack room as she put away her saddle. "Can we talk for a minute?"

"I didn't forget to inject," she protested. "I just got finished with my horse."

He held up his hands in a gesture of surrender. "I get that. I wasn't planning to yell at you."

She pretended to wipe sweat off her forehead. "So what's the problem?"

"There's no problem. I have some good news, in fact."

"The tests were wrong and I don't really have diabetes?"

"Not that good." They came out of the barn and headed down the hill toward the girls' cabin. "I talked with Dr. Vale this morning. She says you can manage your injections on your own. Without supervision."

Lena stopped in her tracks and stared at him. "She does?"

"She believes you understand the risks and you're comfortable enough with the process to take care of yourself."

"Do you agree with her?" She started walking again.

"I know you're smart enough to handle the injections, as long as you don't get distracted or hurry through it. What do you think?"

They reached the steps to the cabin porch and stood for a minute in silence. "I can do it," Lena said finally, nodding. "It's written down, so all I really have to do is follow directions."

"I'll still be checking on you," Garrett warned. "Just because I'm not in the room doesn't mean I won't remember what you're supposed to be doing."

"As if I would be that lucky." To his surprise, she smiled at him. "I might have a question sometimes. Is that okay?"

"Sure." He didn't want to make a big deal of her reliance. "You'd better get going—your team is making lunch."

She shrieked and ran up the steps. "Lizzie will kill me if I'm late!"

Her confidence was encouraging, but Garrett spent the rest of Friday and all of Saturday keeping a close eye on Lena's behavior. At the least sign she wasn't well, he was prepared to step in. He consulted the books Rachel had given him and memorized what to do for both low and high blood-sugar emergencies.

Those emergencies never materialized. By Saturday night, he was beginning to accept that Rachel had been right and Lena could manage her own injections. After two days of constant worry, he was fairly exhausted, and fell into bed at ten o'clock without reading through his sermon for the next morning even once.

He woke up before his alarm and arrived at the church before seven, as usual, to make sure everything was ready for the Sunday service.

As he got out of his truck, he noticed a runner coming down the street from the center of town. She didn't have to get too close before he recognized the red hair and curvy figure, so by the time she reached the church, he was standing at the edge of the yard to greet her.

"That's a great way to enjoy a summer morning."

Rachel slowed and then stopped beside him, breathing only a little fast. "I've been jogging around town since I got here. This was the only direction I hadn't taken." She stared beyond him at the church. "White siding and a gray-shingled steeple. Very traditional."

"Thanks. We try to stick to the basics—love your neighbor as yourself, do unto others…that kind of thing. You could show up again about eleven and check it out."

One eyebrow lifted. "I'd probably get struck by lightning."

He shook his head. "God's more forgiving than that. You can always have a second chance. All you have to do is ask."

"I'll remember." But she didn't sound convinced. "You look quite respectable in your collar and shirt, by the way."

"Only on Sundays. The rest of the week I'm just a cowboy preacher."

"Among other jobs. How's Lena doing?"

"Great. She's taking care of her injections by herself and hasn't seemed to have any problems."

"Are you starting to relax yet?"

Garrett laughed. "I slept pretty well last night. But it's been an adjustment."

Her smile was a welcome sight on a Sunday morning. "It will get easier."

"Equanimity. I remember."

"Right." Rachel glanced at the church again, and then focused on the road. "I'd better finish my run before the sun rises too high."

"Maybe I'll see you later," he suggested. "You'd be welcome to come to the ranch for lunch. We usually eat at one."

She gave him a warning glance. "Probably not."

He grinned as he shrugged. "You can't blame me for trying."

"I wouldn't be too sure about that," she said, and then took off running before he had a chance to reply.

MONDAY MORNING, RACHEL officially opened her office for business.

"Not that I expect a rush of patients at first," she said

to her nurse, Allie Freedman. "But I put a flyer on the bulletin board at Kate's Diner, the feed store and the grocery store, so I hope word will get around."

"It was all the talk at church yesterday," Allie said. "Caroline Donnelly and the Marshall brothers were telling folks that you'd come out to an emergency with one of the kids they're taking care of this summer. They said you'd been checking on her all week long."

"Oh." She swallowed hard. "Well, good word of mouth is always useful."

"Even Pastor Garrett was saying what a blessing it was that you arrived when you did."

Rachel remembered Caroline using that word, as well. "One of the girls at the camp, Lena Smith, has just been diagnosed with diabetes. I urged them to call if they have questions or problems. And I want to order supplies in case of an emergency with Lena—insulin for hyperglycemia and glucagon for hypoglycemia. I'll make a list."

She was at her desk midmorning, going through medical catalogs, when Allie knocked on the office door. "You have a patient," she said, with a wide smile. "Room one."

"Terrific." Heart beating hard, Rachel smoothed her hair, checked to be sure she had her stethoscope in the pocket of her lab coat and then made her way down the hall. Hayley Brewster was the name on the file.

Rachel knocked and entered the room. "Ms. Brewster, it's nice to meet you." She offered her hand. "I'm Dr. Vale. What can I do for you today?" As she shut the door, she noticed a tang of cigarette smoke tinting the air.

The woman took Rachel's hand, although she was also shaking her head. "That's Mrs. Brewster, thank you very much." Tall and thin, she wore jeans and boots and a plaid shirt, with a bandanna tied around her throat. Her silver hair hung in a long braid over her shoulder. "I was

married for fifty-three years and I want people to respect that."

Rachel made a note on the record. "That's quite an accomplishment indeed, Mrs. Brewster. Now, I don't have
your previous medical records yet, so you'll have to fill
me in on your history. I gather that you smoke."

A flush brightened Mrs. Brewster's cheeks. "Occasionally."

"You should quit, you know. As soon as possible."

A lift of one shoulder was the only reply.

So they would move on. "Are you taking any medications?"

The older woman grimaced. "Hell, no, I don't take
medicine. I've got too much to do to waste time being
sick."

"Then why are you here?"

"I heard there was a new doctor in town and I wanted
to come check you out." Mrs. Brewster's eyes were a
piercing gray. "You're not from around here."

"No, I grew up near Laramie."

"You have family there?"

"Um, no. My mother died two years ago." Funny, that
was still so hard to say.

The stern face softened slightly. "My condolences.
What made you decide to come to Bisons Creek?"

"My friend Caroline Donnelly informed me the town
was searching for a doctor and it was exactly the kind of
job I would enjoy."

"That Caroline is a decent girl. Does a lot for the people hereabouts. You've been up at the Circle M this week,
helping with those kids she's taken on. Her and the Marshall boys. They were a handful when they were young,
but they've grown up to be decent men."

"That's certainly my impression."

"You're not married."

"No."

"You could do worse than one of the Marshalls."

Rachel laughed. "I'm not considering marriage right now, Mrs. Brewster. And if there's nothing I can do for you—"

"We'll be having a party," Mrs. Brewster said. "Was talking to Pastor Garrett about it yesterday at church." The gray gaze narrowed. "You weren't in church."

She didn't hesitate. "I don't go to church."

"Well, at least you're honest about it. Anyway, we'll be having this get-together for the town to meet you. Seven p.m., Friday night, at my place." With a nod, she walked to the door. "See you then."

"Thanks…" Rachel said, as her patient left the room. She wasn't sure whether to be amused or simply stunned by Hayley Brewster's visit. She'd never expected to be the one being examined during an office call.

As for the party invitation—she detected the crafty mind of Garrett Marshall behind that plan. Using his parishioners to spread the word about her practice and then enlisting them to create an official welcome was a wily way of involving her with his church. At least Hayley Brewster hadn't pressured her when she said she didn't attend services. Rachel doubted she would escape so easily with all of the faithful.

She was certain Garrett meant well, though, and she would cooperate with his plan, because it suited her own ends. What better way to advertise her practice than with a pleasant Friday evening spent meeting her future patients?

As for today, however, she was supposed to be at the Circle M Ranch at noon for the teenagers' first lesson in first aid. She had no idea what to expect from the kids—

would they cooperate, or be bored by the idea? She'd tried to come up with some entertaining aspects to emergency response, but what Thomas and Marcos would consider fun was more than she could predict.

And then there was the possibility of meeting up with Garrett again. Their encounter on Sunday had stuck with her all day—he'd come across as so serious and…and *faithful* in his clerical shirt and collar. No less attractive, though, which was the problem. The differences between them—her in running clothes, sweaty and winded— couldn't have been more apparent. She'd gone to Kate's Diner for lunch, only to spend most of the meal remembering the night she'd come there with him.

"I'll be back about two," she told Allie as she left the office. "If there's an emergency, of course, call me. If someone comes in, schedule an appointment for later this afternoon. All right?"

"Perfect. Have fun—I hear those kids are a handful."

"That's what I'm afraid of."

"You'll do fine."

Watching the kids during lunch, Rachel wasn't so sure. Caroline said they'd spent the morning cleaning saddles and bridles—nobody's idea of fun. So they all seemed grumpy as they made their own sandwiches and sat down at the long table in the bunkhouse to eat. None of the Marshall brothers were present, and Rachel didn't ask where Garrett was. Out of sight, out of mind…she hoped.

But since he wasn't around, she thought she'd better keep an eye on Lena, just to be safe. "Did you test before lunch?" she asked the girl as she passed by. "Take your insulin?"

Lena rolled her eyes. "Of course."

"Just checking," Rachel said with a smile. "I'd probably forget constantly."

"No, you wouldn't." Lena didn't lighten up. "Not with people warning you you'll go blind or die if you don't." She brushed by Rachel and went to sit with Justino.

"Reality is setting in," Caroline commented. "She's been difficult since she got up this morning. Bit Garrett's head off when he asked if she'd done her injection and argued with him about which cereal she should eat."

Rachel nodded. "I'll call the nurse educator and suggest they talk about food choices when Lena goes for her appointment this week. She can't solve all her problems with insulin—she has to eat well, too. That white bread sandwich isn't the best option. At least you offered whole wheat."

"Susannah has been planning the menus and reading up on healthy choices for kids with diabetes. We're all trying to help."

"Lena probably realizes that, though she won't admit it." Rachel noticed that most of the kids were finished eating. "Shall I get started with first aid?"

"As soon as we get the table cleared off." The process of cleaning up generated some grumbles, but in a few minutes Rachel found herself facing seven faces ranging in expression from indifference to outright disdain.

"Why do I have to take first-aid lessons?" Marcos snorted as she passed out the manuals she'd brought for each of the kids. "I'm not going to be no doctor."

"First aid isn't about being a doctor. It's about what to do when there's an emergency. What does the word *rescuer* mean?" She wrote the word at the top of the whiteboard she'd brought along.

"Hero," Thomas said.

"Could be. What does a rescuer do?"

Lizzie raised her hand. "Helps somebody?"

Rachel smiled at her. "Right. And first aid is about

knowing what to do in case of an emergency. What kind of situation would that be?"

"A car wreck," Thomas said.

"A motorcycle crash," Marcos added.

Thomas sneered at him. "That's the same thing."

"A bike crash is not the same as a car wreck," Marcos insisted. "You get hurt worse in a bike crash."

"That's stupid. You can get killed in a car."

"Right," Rachel said forcefully, writing both items down. "Let's get some other examples of situations when people need help."

The list grew with suggestions from the others, including avalanche, tsunami and shark attack, as well as more relevant situations, including falling from a horse and hitting your head on a rock.

Leading the kids through the first chapters of the manual, Rachel was encouraged that most of them participated, though Marcos sat with his arms folded and a sneer on his face through the whole lesson. Nate was quiet but provided enough answers to prove he was keeping up with the material. Lena and Justino put their phones down, which constituted a major victory.

But before they became bored, she wanted to get them out of their chairs. "Suppose you go for a hike in the mountains with a couple of friends. You're enjoying yourselves, but then suddenly one of your friends steps wrong and sprains their ankle. Now they can't walk, but you have to get them to the parking lot for the ride home. What can you do?"

Marcos grinned. "Leave them to be eaten by bears."

Rachel nodded. "That's an option. Anything else?"

"Make a crutch?" Lena suggested.

"You could, if you had tools and supplies. Here's another possibility. You could carry them to the parking lot."

"Yeah, right," Thomas said. "I can picture the girls carrying some guy down the trail."

"If you have two people, it can be done with what's called the two-handed seat carry. Choose a partner, and we'll practice this technique."

The kids paired up as expected—Becky with Lizzie and Justino with Lena, leaving Nate, Thomas and Marcos avoiding each other's eyes. Rachel took Marcos by the hand. "You're with me, and Nate, you're with Thomas. Face each other and with one hand, clasp your partner's arm above their wrist." She demonstrated with Marcos. "The other person takes hold of you the same way. Now put your other hand on the person's shoulder, and theirs on yours. Right. This way, you have a place where a person could sit down and be transported for a fairly long distance."

"And I'll test each one," Garrett said, grinning as he joined them. "If you drop me, you're in serious trouble."

Chapter Seven

Garrett saw Rachel's eyes widen in surprise. She'd been so focused on the teenagers she hadn't noticed his arrival.

"Right." She took a deep breath. "Mr. Garrett will be the victim. Try carrying him from the table to the far side of the room."

"You're too heavy," Thomas said. "The girls will drop you."

"We will not." Becky brushed her pigtails behind her shoulders. "We could totally rescue somebody if we had to."

"None of us is strong enough." Marcos let go of Rachel's arm. "You're gonna fall flat on your butt every time."

"Have a little faith," Garrett said, approaching Thomas and Nate. "Here we go, guys. Hold tight."

Pair by pair, the kids tried out the carry, and were surprised when they were able to support his weight. "I can't believe it." Thomas shook his head. "Even the girls can do it."

Marcos and Rachel were the last to go. "Come on, Marcos." Rachel held out her hands. "We're as strong as everybody else."

He eyed her warily. "I don't know about that." But

he grabbed her arm and put his hand on her shoulder. "Okay. I guess."

"Ready if you are," Garrett said, standing facing away from them. "Go for it."

They walked up behind him. "Sit," Rachel said. "We've got you."

As he bent his knees, they supported his thighs with their clasped hands and moved their arms down to cradle his back. He let his full weight rest in their hold— and didn't fall.

"Way to go," he said, when they set him on his feet. "Now we can try the three-person hammock carry."

Rachel stared at him. "You're awfully well informed."

Smiling, he winked at her. "I've taken first aid. I still have the manual. So show us how this works."

The kids clamored to learn the carry, so she gave them instructions, with Garrett again acting as their victim. For this exercise, he lay on the floor and three teenagers picked him up with an arm under his neck, his chest and waist, his butt and thighs. They worked in different combinations, including just the three girls, and all were successful in carrying him across the floor.

"Well done," he said, getting to his feet after the last trio had finished. "I feel safer already having you guys around."

Judging by the teenagers' energy level, Rachel wouldn't get their attention again this afternoon. "That's it for today," she said loudly. "Tomorrow we'll talk about bugs and snakes."

"I hate snakes." Becky shuddered. "They're so creepy and slithery."

"What about spiders?" Lizzie asked. "I've seen spiders everywhere out here."

"Some of them are poisonous," Thomas told her with relish. "They bite you and you die."

"Which ones?"

"I'll have pictures tomorrow," Rachel said. "Don't worry about it tonight. Most spiders are not poisonous."

"On the other hand, the snakes we run into…" Garrett grinned.

Rachel frowned at him. "Don't get them started. You're the one who'll have to deal with Lizzie's nightmares tonight."

"Or to be more precise, Caroline will be." He followed her over to the table and watched her erase the whiteboard. "You first session seemed to be a success. They were all participating, as far as I could tell."

"I'm trying not to bore them with too much detail. Just a general overview." She moved the board on its easel out of the way. "Hayley Brewster came to the clinic this morning."

"Is she sick? She was fine yesterday at church."

"Just checking me out, she said. And she invited me to a welcome party on Friday night." She looked at him askance. "I take it that was your idea?"

"That depends on how upset you are."

She gave him a sunny smile. "Not at all. It's a great way for me to meet my future patients."

"Well, then, I claim responsibility for the whole plan. I'll be doing all the cooking, too."

"Now *that* I don't believe." She gathered her papers together. "I'd better make an appearance soon at the clinic in case someone else stops in. Thanks for your participation in today's activity. Having you to carry made it more fun for them than carrying each other."

"I'm glad I could help." He walked with her to her car. "How was Lena at lunch?"

"Resistant. She doesn't want any interference."

"I got the same treatment at breakfast, which makes trusting her more difficult."

"All you can do is keep an eye on her behavior. Either low or high blood sugar could be a problem if she's not dosing properly. I'm sure it's difficult to watch her with six other kids to monitor. And she might try to hide the fact that she's not well."

"I understand. We're handling this." She opened her car door and climbed in, but he held the panel so she couldn't close it. "Have you noticed," he said, "that all we ever talk about is Lena? Or maybe the other kids?"

Her brows drew together. "That's what we have in common, Garrett. That's why we see each other."

He shook his head, rejecting that explanation. "You never did reveal what kind of books you read."

She eyed him with exasperation. "Westerns and mysteries," she said. "There are some really excellent writers these days setting their mysteries in the West. I love those."

Garrett grinned. "Tony Hillerman and Craig Johnson—I've read their books. They're great. But I'm a fan of traditional Westerns, too—Louis L'Amour and Zane Grey."

"I've read them all." Enthusiasm brightened her eyes. "Sometimes I try to choose a favorite, but there are too many wonderful titles to pick just one."

"Are you a country music fan?"

"Classic country, definitely. Though I enjoy some of the newer songs, too."

"So what's your idea of a perfect rainy afternoon?"

Rachel laughed. "Reading a Western with George Jones on the radio, of course. And a bowl of buttered popcorn to snack on. What's yours?"

"I'd go for ice cream instead of popcorn."

FREE Merchandise is 'in the Cards' for you!

Dear Reader,

We're giving away FREE MERCHANDISE!

Seriously, we'd like to reward you for reading this novel by giving you **FREE MERCHANDISE** worth over $20 retail. And no purchase is necessary!

It's easy! All you have to do is look inside for your Free Merchandise Voucher. Return the Voucher promptly...and we'll send you valuable Free Merchandise!

Thanks again for reading one of our novels—and enjoy your Free Merchandise with our compliments!

Pam Powers

Pam Powers

P.S. Look inside to see what Free Merchandise is **"in the cards"** for you!

We'd like to send you two free books like the one you are enjoying now. Your two books have a combined price of over $10 retail, but they are yours to keep absolutely FREE! We'll even send you 2 wonderful surprise gifts. You can't lose!

REMEMBER: Your Free Merchandise, consisting of **2 Free Books** and **2 Free Gifts**, is worth over $20 retail! No purchase is necessary, so please send for your Free Merchandise today.

YOUR FREE MERCHANDISE INCLUDES...

2 FREE Books **AND** 2 FREE Mystery Gifts

FREE MERCHANDISE VOUCHER

❑ Please send my Free Merchandise, consisting of
2 Free Books and **2 Free Mystery Gifts**.
I understand that I am under no obligation to buy
anything, as explained on the back of this card.

154/354 HDL GKAU

Please Print

FIRST NAME

LAST NAME

ADDRESS

APT.#   CITY

STATE/PROV.   ZIP/POSTAL CODE

Offer limited to one per household and not applicable to series that subscriber is currently receiving.
Your Privacy—The Reader Service is committed to protecting your privacy. Our Privacy Policy is available online at www.ReaderService.com or upon request from the Reader Service. We make a portion of our mailing list available to reputable third parties that offer products we believe may interest you. If you prefer that we not exchange your name with third parties, or if you wish to clarify or modify your communication preferences, please visit us at www.ReaderService.com/consumerschoice or write to us at Reader Service Preference Service, P.O. Box 9062, Buffalo, NY 14240-9062. Include your complete name and address.

NO PURCHASE NECESSARY!

AR-516-FMH16

▶ Detach card and mail today. No stamp needed.

© 2015 HARLEQUIN ENTERPRISES LIMITED ● ® and ™ are trademarks owned and used by the trademark owner and/or its licensee. Printed in the U.S.A.

READER SERVICE—Here's how it works:

Accepting your 2 free Harlequin® American Romance® books and 2 free gifts (gifts valued at approximately $10.00) places you under no obligation to buy anything. You may keep the books and gifts and return the shipping statement marked "cancel." If you do not cancel, about a month later we'll send you 4 additional books and bill you just $4.74 each in the U.S. or $5.49 each in Canada. That is a savings of at least 12% off the cover price. It's quite a bargain! Shipping and handling is just 50¢ per book in the U.S. and 75¢ per book in Canada.* You may cancel at any time, but if you choose to continue, every month we'll send you 4 more books, which you may either purchase at the discount price or return to us and cancel your subscription. *Terms and prices subject to change without notice. Prices do not include applicable taxes. Sales tax applicable in N.Y. Canadian residents will be charged applicable taxes. Offer not valid in Quebec. Books received may not be as shown. All orders subject to approval. Credit or debit balances in a customer's account(s) may be offset by any other outstanding balance owed by or to the customer. Please allow 4 to 6 weeks for delivery. Offer available while quantities last.

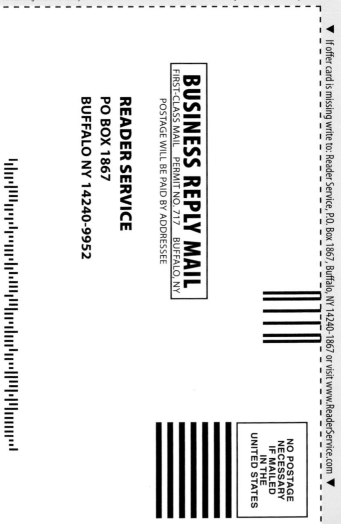

"Then I don't have to share." She caught her breath. "I mean, if…" The picture she'd drawn hung in the air between them—the two of them spending a rainy afternoon together cuddled side by side on the sofa, reading.

"I like the idea," Garrett said, giving her a wink. "We'll have to try it one of these days. But for now I'll let you be on your way."

Before she could come up with a reply, he shut the door. Rachel sat for a moment, flustered. Finally, shaking her head, she reversed her SUV, circled and headed down the drive. Garrett waved and then watched until she'd gone out of sight.

If he could keep her off balance, he decided as he walked to the barn, he might be able to make some progress. When she wasn't on guard against him, they were good together. Eventually she'd admit that. He'd simply have to keep surprising her.

At the top of the hill, he found some of the teenagers lounging on hay bales inside the barn, playing with their phones. Lizzie and Becky had gone out to practice running barrels with Caroline, and Nate usually went for a solo ride in the afternoon.

"How about some bucking practice?" Garrett suggested. "It's not too hot today."

But Thomas only shrugged. "Is that all we're ever gonna do? Ride that dumb barrel?"

"I want to ride a real bull," Marcos said, still wearing the bandage around his head. "I thought we were going to do an actual rodeo."

Garrett leaned against the door frame. "You figure you're ready to sit on a live animal?"

"Why not?" Marcos got to his feet. "How can we know if we don't try?"

Thomas stood beside him. "Don't you have some bulls we can ride?"

Garrett shook his head. "You are definitely not ready for bulls. The most we would try would be steers. That's what your age group rides in the junior rodeo."

"Could we do that?" Lena joined the chorus. "I want to ride a steer."

Garrett didn't like the idea, but this wasn't the right time for an argument about what she could and couldn't do. "I'll have to talk to Ford and Wyatt and Caroline. For now, though, keep practicing. Thomas, you're up first."

Lena wanted to ride the barrel, too. Garrett was reluctant, but she seemed to be feeling fine, so he didn't protest.

Then it became obvious to Garrett that the boys were not pulling the ropes as hard for Lena as they did for each other. She kept yelling at them, "More. More!"

Thomas and Marcos took the girl at her word and began to jerk the ropes with greater and greater effort. Lena stayed on for a few seconds, but then Marcos gave a big pull and she tumbled off onto her side.

Garrett rushed over to kneel beside her. He put a hand on her shoulder. "Are you all right?"

"Sure." She rolled to her back, laughing. "That was the best ride ever. You guys make it too easy," she told the boys. "That's not fair."

"Well, now it's my turn," Marcos declared.

Garrett gave Lena a hand up from the ground. "Maybe you ought to test your blood sugar," he said in a low voice. "To be sure you're okay."

She rolled her eyes. "I just tested before lunch."

"Exercise can affect your results. Why don't you do a quick check?"

"Because I'm not making a big deal of this." She

marched over to the barrel and took hold of the rope Marcos had used. "Let's watch you ride, Marcos. Come on."

Short of taking her by the arm and marching her to the cabin, Garrett couldn't force Lena to do a blood test. And he wasn't sure even that would work.

"I lost that battle," he said when he called Rachel later in the afternoon. "But I don't know what I could have done differently. How do you convince a teenager to take care of herself?"

"I understand why you'd be frustrated." Her ready empathy soothed his concern. "She's probably going to have to experience some negative consequences before she accepts the importance of testing regularly. When is her appointment in Buffalo?"

"Thursday."

"They should talk to her about exercise and diabetes, make it clear how activity can affect her glucose level. You don't have to bear the entire burden of her care, Garrett. You're part of a team."

"I'm grateful to have your support, at least." He didn't want to let her go without some personal conversation between them. "How was your afternoon? More patients?"

"Terri, from the diner, brought in her six-year-old, who has tonsillitis. A couple of others. It's a start." She paused, and he expected her to end the conversation. "What's on the camp schedule the rest of the day?" she asked, instead. "How do you keep them busy?"

He smiled into his phone. "Right now they've got a break, which they mostly spend on their phones. Some of them read. Then there's dinner to cook, eat and clean up. Tonight we're taking them out for a campfire in the woods." He chose to push his luck. "Care to join us? It's a special experience, shared with friends under the stars."

There was a moment of silence. "Yes," she said finally. "I'd enjoy that. What time should I be there?"

They settled the details and disconnected, but Garrett was still grinning when he strolled into the house. Ford and Wyatt were at the dining table going over insurance paperwork.

"What are you so happy about?" Wyatt asked. "I could sure use something to smile over after all this mess."

"Rachel is coming to the campfire tonight." He sat at the end of the table.

"Aha. I thought you had a special gleam in your eye when she was here," Ford said. "Pursuing the lady doctor, are you?"

"Doing my best, but she's quite a challenge."

"Shall we sing love songs tonight, provide a suitable soundtrack for romance?"

"With seven teenagers sitting around, I doubt there'll be any romance. I'm just trying to get within arm's reach."

"Of what?" Caroline asked, coming into the room. She put her hands on Ford's shoulders and leaned in to kiss his cheek.

"Your friend," Ford said. "He's fallen for Rachel Vale."

Caroline stared at him, her brows drawn together. "I can see that. You would be good for Rachel—your positive attitude could bring more lightness into her life. She tends to be too serious."

"Does that mean I have your approval?"

She held up a cautioning finger. "As long as you don't hurt her."

"Believe me," Garrett said, "The way things are going, I'm much more likely to be the one who ends up getting hurt."

IN HINDSIGHT, RACHEL couldn't believe she'd agreed to go the campfire at the Circle M. Yes, she'd spent the past couple of nights alone in her apartment, cleaning and scrubbing until the paint peeled, vacuuming so often the carpet had started to unravel. And, sure, the idea of spending an evening outside under the Wyoming stars seemed the perfect way to end the day.

But… Garrett Marshall.

She'd be meeting him in an undeniably romantic setting, without any way to defend herself against his charisma. How hard could she make things on herself?

Of course the teenagers would be present, along with his brothers and Caroline. So there would be no possibility for a repetition of those kisses in the kitchen, the ones that tended to preoccupy her mind when she wasn't being careful. Sleep had been elusive the past two nights, and filled with restless dreams when it finally did arrive, which made deliberately choosing to enjoy his company an even crazier idea.

Nevertheless, she dressed in her nice jeans and a long-sleeved shirt and made her way out to the ranch. She arrived just as the kids emerged from the bunkhouse and joined them beside a pickup truck with high sides to the bed, which had been filled with bales of hay.

"There you are." Garrett came around the rear of the vehicle. "Obviously, it's a hayride. Come aboard." He held her hand as she climbed onto the bumper of the truck and then clambered in after her. "Here's a nice sturdy bale." They sat down together, their hips and the sides of their thighs touching. "Ford's driving, so we're in steady hands."

The truck bed was crowded with the teenagers, plus Susannah Bradley and her daughter. "This is scratchy stuff," Amber said. "I don't want to sit here."

"Sit on my lap," Garrett said. "I'm not scratchy."

Amber crawled across the hay and onto his knees. He wrapped his arms around her waist to hold her steady.

"That's better," she announced. She looked over at Rachel. "I like Mr. Garrett. He tells good stories."

"Does he? What kind of stories?"

"Bible stories. They're in-intersting. Do you tell stories?"

"I haven't had anybody to tell stories to."

"You can tell me a story."

"Right now?"

She nodded vigorously, her curls bouncing around her head.

"Um…well…"

"Once upon a time," Amber prompted.

"Once upon a time," Rachel said, frantically searching her brain for a plot, "there was a lady who…who traveled to a new country where she didn't know anybody."

"Why did she go there?"

"She wanted to start a shop. Selling…um…"

"Medicines," Garrett said. "That she made herself."

"Right." She'd take all the help she could get. "One day when she was traveling through this new country, she came to a little cottage which would be perfect for her shop. When she knocked on the door, an elf opened it."

"With pointed ears?" Amber asked.

Rachel nodded. "An elf with pointed ears. He was busy hammering nails, painting walls and making the shop ready to be used. But when the lady asked him if she could sell her medicines there, he insisted she would have to undertake three quests before he would allow her inside."

Amber clapped her hands. "I like quests."

A lucky guess. "Well, the elf told the lady that her first quest would be to bring him an apple from the orchard of the witch who lived in the nearby forest. Her apples gave extra kindness to all who ate them, but the witch refused to share them with anyone. So the lady set out—"

"What's her name?" Amber asked.

"Oh...um, Melody."

The little girl nodded. "That's pretty."

"So Melody set out to find the witch's house in the middle of the forest. The path was dangerous, with bears lurking in the shadows, snakes coiled in her way, and a huge swamp to cross filled with hungry alligators and sharp-toothed fish."

Amber's eyes were wide with expectation. Rachel glanced around and saw that the other kids were listening, too.

She swallowed hard and continued. "Melody managed to avoid the bears and the snakes, and she crossed the swamp to find the witch's house. But when she asked the witch for an apple, the witch said, 'You'll have to do something for me first. You'll have to weed my garden before the sun goes down. Then I'll give you an apple.'

"The garden around the house was such a mess, Melody didn't believe she could possibly make it neat in a week, much less an afternoon. She was determined to try, however, and she set to work. Soon she realized she had helpers—the birds and the deer who lived in the forest came out to assist her in cleaning up the weeds. By the time the sun started to set, the place was neat and tidy. When the witch saw her garden, she was amazed, and she gave Melody a basket of apples to carry with her, plus a charm to keep away all danger on the way through the woods."

"I bet the elf was mad about that," Amber said.

"He was definitely not happy when Melody brought him a whole basket of apples. 'Well,' he said, 'the second quest is much more difficult. You must go to the wizard who lives in a cave by the river and bring me...'" Rachel hesitated, at a loss.

"A bottle of the Water of Knowledge," Lizzie suggested.

Rachel smiled at her. "Exactly. The Water of Knowledge. When she asked the wizard for the Water of Knowledge, he said that first she would have to clean his cave, including the floor, which was covered with dirt."

At that moment, the truck angled off the smooth road they'd been traveling and onto a narrow track. The ride suddenly got much rougher as they drove over ruts and rocks. Pine trees now loomed on both sides, blocking out the sun.

"How did she clean the cave?" Amber had the most secure seat of them all, on Garrett's lap. Everyone else was getting bounced around.

"The river rose up over its banks," Rachel said, "and scoured all the dirt out of the cave, leaving the stone floor and walls shining. The wizard was so impressed, he had no choice but to give Melody a bottle of the Water of Knowledge."

With a jerk, the truck came to a stop. "We've arrived," Garrett said, letting go of Amber. "Welcome to Fort Marshall." He jumped to the ground and turned to lift the little girl down, then held a hand out to Rachel. "Careful, now."

With her hand in his she jumped, very conscious of the contact between his skin and hers. She pulled away quickly. "Fort Marshall?"

He helped Susannah down and then the three girls. "Wyatt discovered this place when we were teenagers. Mr. MacPherson didn't know about it. We made it into our private retreat."

On one side of the clearing, a wide creek rushed and tumbled over its rocky bed, bordered by large boulders, some the size of small cars. Nearby, a plateau of wide, flat stones created the perfect setting for a campfire, with the open sky above and plenty of room for gathering near the flames.

The kids had scattered across the area, exploring the possibilities. Lizzie and Becky stood on the edge of the dense forest, staring into the darkness within. Nate and Amber were collecting pebbles on a narrow strip of sand at the edge of the stream, while Marcos and Thomas had started climbing the bigger rocks. Justino and Lena sat together, totally immersed in each other, as usual.

Following Garrett's lead, Rachel carried an armload of firewood from the truck to the fire circle, where Ford had begun building what resembled a tepee of sticks.

She set down her logs and brushed off her shirt. "Is this the same creek where we had the picnic last week?"

"Another branch of it," he said. "But both spots are part of Crazy Woman Creek."

"That sounds as if there's a legend involved."

Garrett nodded. "A white woman had her family killed by Native Americans."

"Or—" Dylan brought another load of logs "—a Native woman had her family killed by whites. Take your pick."

"Is there a third option?" Rachel asked. "Maybe an old woman living on her own who mixed up strange medicine brews?"

"Or who ran a still and sold moonshine," Garrett said with a wink.

"Excellent! We can rewrite the mythology." Sharing the laughter of the moment, Rachel found her gaze caught by his. His kindness and good nature, the warmth of his smile and the encouragement in his eyes, all urged her to drop her defenses and accept the closeness he offered.

"Thomas, Marcos! Come back this way. It's getting too dark to go so far."

At the sound of Caroline's voice, Garrett frowned and looked away, breaking their connection. "What's the problem? Where did they escape to?"

Caroline stood by the creek with her hands on her hips, clearly exasperated. "Upstream. I can't even be sure they heard me call. No, wait, Thomas is coming." They watched as the boy negotiated his way across the biggest boulders until he finally reached the smaller stones and could climb down to the ground.

"There's this pool up there," he said, his tan face flushed with excitement and exertion. "It has frogs and fish and stuff in it. It's really neat."

"But where's Marcos?" Caroline asked. "Why didn't he come with you?"

Thomas shrugged. "He's being stupid. Said he'd come when he was ready."

"I'll fetch him." Garrett pushed up his shirtsleeves. "We don't want him scrambling around on the rocks in the dark." Though it was still light in the clearing, the shadows between the trees had lengthened.

"You're going to climb after him?" Rachel put a hand on his arm. "There's not another way around?"

He shook his head. "Don't worry—when we came out here as kids, we'd take our poles up to that pool to catch the fish. They were always too smart for us, of course, but it was fun trying. I remember the way. I'll be fine."

Setting a foot on a low stone, he started to scale the nearest boulder, his movements sure and steady. Rachel watched as he crossed from rock to rock, crouching low in places to use his hands for balance, gripping a tree here or a shrub there to make his way across a gap. As far as she could tell, he didn't take a single misstep.

"He really does know the way," she said to Caroline, when he'd disappeared from sight. "They must have come here often as boys."

"Ford says they did. They certainly enjoy these nights out, and the kids do, too. Wyatt hates having to miss the campfires. But his back just isn't ready for the roughness of the road."

"He's smart to be careful. Spine injuries are tricky, and I'm sure he wants to heal properly."

Caroline chuckled. "Mostly, he's just dying to get back in the saddle. If we'd allow it, he'd probably try riding tomorrow."

"Men hate being out of commission."

"Isn't that the truth? They believe they're immortal. Just like teenagers. Oh, look, there's Marcos. And Garrett behind him."

Marcos came slowly over the rocks, occasionally uncertain about which move to make next. Garrett spoke to him a couple of times, perhaps offering advice or encouragement. The boy hesitated at the top of the biggest and last boulder, staring down at the ground but evidently unsure of how to get there.

Garrett didn't push him forward but waited patiently for Marcos to dredge up his own courage. And he did, finally, with a grin that signaled pride in his accomplishment.

"Good job," Garrett said when he came down himself with a few quick, confident steps. "Now you can go sit in the truck." Marcos stalked off, scowling. "I figured he needed an immediate consequence," he said to Rachel. "He won't enjoy tonight after disobeying Caroline."

The sky above the trees had darkened to a dusky blue,

bringing twilight to the clearing. Ford's fire had started up nicely, its cheerful crackling an invitation to sit near the flames.

"Can I offer you a seat?" Garrett gestured to a place on the circle.

"You must have some great memories of being here," Rachel said as he sat down beside her. "This kind of experience would be hard to forget."

"We spent many a night rolled up in our sleeping bags, watching the stars. Or telling ghost stories—Ford was the best at making up scary tales. We didn't always have it easy after our parents died, but we stuck together. So, yeah, we've got lots of great times to look back on. And we're still having them." His gaze rested on her face. "What about you?"

"Me?" She watched as a log fell and sparks shot up out of the fire.

"What do you remember about your teenage years?"

Chapter Eight

Rachel didn't answer for so long that Garrett had almost decided she wasn't going to.

"My mom worked two jobs," she said at last, still staring at the fire. "And she was sick a lot. But sometimes, when she had a Saturday or a Sunday off, we would get in the car and just drive. Up into the mountains or out over the plains, for hours, singing along with the radio. She didn't care if I couldn't carry a tune, because she couldn't, either. We'd turn the volume all the way up, roll the windows down and enjoy ourselves."

Garrett grinned. "Sounds like a terrific experience."

She nodded. "We'd stop to eat in some diner or truck stop, and she'd always ignore her diet and order the cheeseburger and onion rings. 'You only live once,' she'd say, and enjoy every bite. Then we'd drive home by a different route, just to see what could be seen. It was such a sense of freedom, driving with no destination, only the potential of the unknown ahead. I loved those days."

"That's quite a gift to give a child—a sense of freedom and possibility."

"She was certain I'd go to medical school, though the prospects, when you're living on the edge of poverty, aren't promising. And she was always sure her newest boyfriend would be the prince she'd been waiting for.

My mom was a great one for believing in possibilities. Or, for that matter, impossibilities."

At last we're getting somewhere. Garrett waited, hoping she would say more.

Then he saw Amber making her careful way across the fire circle, being sure to stay well away from the flames. She came to stand in front of Rachel.

"Can you finish the story?" she asked.

Rachel cleared her throat. "Now might not be the best time…"

But the teenagers encouraged her. "Please finish," Becky said.

Nate, who rarely said anything, agreed. "We want the third quest."

Before she could start, however, Amber turned around and then backed up to sit herself down in Rachel's lap. "Now you can tell the story," the little girl said.

"Okay, then," the doctor said, laughing. "Where was I?"

Lizzie answered. "The wizard gave her his magic boat to get across the river."

"Right. Melody took the bottle of the Water of Knowledge to the elf in the cottage. He, of course, was very unhappy that she'd completed the second quest. 'The third quest is the hardest of all,' he warned her. 'You must go to the dragon who lives in the mountains and return with the fire from his throat.'"

Garrett was reasonably sure that Rachel had never told a fairy tale to a five-year-old before, let alone a group of teenagers and adults. But she made good work of the story, detailing the heroine's journey through the treacherous mountains populated with ravenous lions and evil gnomes. After fighting through an avalanche, she reached the dragon's lair and came face-to-face with the monster himself.

"What color is the dragon?" Amber wanted to know.

Rachel had learned a trick or two this evening. "What color should he be?"

"Purple. With shiny green eyes."

"So Melody asked the purple dragon for some of his fire to light the lantern she'd brought with her. But—"

"She has to do something first." Amber rested her head against Rachel's shoulder. "What does she have to do?"

Rachel explained that Melody would have to count all of the dragon's gold coins, which filled up most of his cavern. And she would have to do it before nightfall. Fortunately, an army of ants came to her aid, and she counted all the coins in the time allowed. Pleased to learn just how much gold he had, the dragon breathed on her lantern and gave her a flame to take to the elf, along with a coat that made her invisible to the lions and the gnomes.

"Unfortunately," Rachel said, "the coat couldn't protect her against the rain, which fell as she traveled through the mountains. Melody spent the whole night huddled over the lantern, hoping to keep the storm from putting out the flame. She almost despaired, but in the morning, just before dawn, the rain stopped and she saw that the fire from the dragon still burned.

"She carried the lantern to the elf. 'Now you have the Apples of Kindness,' he said, 'the Water of Knowledge and the Fire of Skill. These three gifts will make you a wise medicine woman for all who seek your help.' Then he vanished in a puff of smoke, leaving Melody free to use the cottage as she wished." Rachel paused a moment. "The end."

Someone—probably Caroline—started to applaud,

and the teenagers quickly joined in, adding their own approving comments. "Excellent!"

"All right!" and even, "Not bad," from Thomas.

Their storyteller held up a hand. "I'm glad you all enjoyed it. But I know someone else who has vanished." She glanced down at Amber. "Into sleep."

Susannah started to stand. "I'll take her—"

"I'll hold her till we leave," Rachel said. "There's no sense in waking her up now."

Garrett liked how she looked with a child in her arms but doubted that she would appreciate the sentiment. "How about some music?" he asked Ford instead.

Rachel's delight showed in her face. "We get to have music? That's terrific!"

In fact, he learned over the next hour just how much Rachel Vale loved music, as Ford played his guitar and the kids sang along. She knew the rap lyrics and pop tunes the kids liked, as well as the old standards and folk songs they'd grown up with. And, no, she couldn't carry a tune, but she hummed anyway—quietly, for Amber's benefit.

"Your family has more than its share of talent," she commented after a rousing rendition of "On Top of Spaghetti." "All of you sing, and Ford plays, as well. I'm quite impressed."

"And you tell stories, so we're even."

She winced. "It wasn't really a very good story. I've never done it off the top of my head before."

"Hey, you kept their interest, which is what matters. But at this point, unless I'm very much mistaken, it's time for—"

Thomas called out across the general conversation. "Can we have s'mores now?"

Garrett got to his feet. "I'll be right back." He returned

from the truck with a basket containing the evening's snack. Walking around the circle, he handed each person a small plastic bag filled with the treat Susannah had prepared—a combination of cereals, dried fruits, nuts and chocolate candies. "We're trying something different tonight."

Thomas stared at the bag with suspicion. "What is this, rabbit food?"

"Trail mix," Garrett explained. "It's good. And good for you."

"No s'mores?" Lizzie asked. "Really?"

"Taste this," Caroline suggested. "It's got chocolate in it."

"We always have s'mores." Nate held his bag without opening it. "Why the change?"

"Because of me." Lena stood up. "You did this because of me."

Garrett faced her. "It doesn't hurt any of us to try a different, less sugary snack for once."

"You didn't trust me to make the right choice," she said. "You figured I would eat a s'more."

"I hoped this would make the right choice easier for you."

"And now you've ruined the campfire for everybody and it's my fault." She stomped across the fire circle and threw her plastic bag in the basket. Tears streaked her cheeks. "They all hate me because they can't have s'mores. Thanks a lot."

Crying in earnest, Lena strode away from the firelight. When she reached the truck, Marcos shone his flashlight to help her climb in the back, where she sat as far from him as she could manage.

Garrett blew out a short breath. "Okay. Eat up, everybody. Then we'll sing some more."

But the heart had gone out of the evening. Ford tried to get some songs going but ended up in a trio with Caroline and Dylan while the kids sat mute. A short while later, Garrett doused the fire and ushered the teenagers into the truck for the drive to the ranch. Unlike previous campfire trips, there was no cheerful chatter on the way, no flashlight duels. In the face of such resistance, even the adults were quiet.

Once they reached the barn, the kids dispersed without the usual curfew protests. The first to get down, Lena headed directly toward the girls' cabin. Justino tried to follow her, but she shook her head and waved him away. He stood staring after her, as if she might relent. When she didn't, he slowly trailed the other boys into the bunkhouse and closed the door.

Standing beside the truck with his brothers, Caroline and Rachel, Garrett rubbed a hand over his face. "That was a disaster. Who could guess s'mores would be such a big deal?" When no one said anything, he answered himself. "I should have, obviously. It was my mistake and I have to fix it. But how?"

"Maybe you should go in and talk to Lena," Caroline said. "Explain you were just trying to make things easier for her. Now that she's calmed down, you could get through."

He looked at Rachel. "What do you think? Is she ready to listen?"

"I doubt it." Her smile was rueful. "She still seemed pretty angry to me. And she's trying to deal with Lizzie and Becky, working out whether they hate her or not. Give her a while to ponder what happened on her own. Some independent reflection will be helpful for her."

"She's the one who behaved badly," Ford pointed out. "Not you. She owes you an apology."

"Do teenagers apologize?" Dylan shrugged a shoulder. "I haven't witnessed much of that around here lately."

"There's always a first time." Caroline sighed. "But I know what you mean. They focus on their own reactions without considering the effect their behavior might have on someone else."

"So I shouldn't hold my breath," Garrett said. "I'll try to talk to her tomorrow morning. Maybe we can come to an understanding after a night's sleep."

"Meanwhile, I'll go make sure the girls are getting along." Caroline turned toward the cabin. "Thanks for coming, Rachel. See you tomorrow."

"I'll check on the boys before I come in," Ford said, going with her. Holding hands, they headed down the hill.

"You could ask Lena if she did her injection," Garrett called after them. "Just to be sure."

"So she can be mad at me, too?" she called. "Thanks."

Garrett met Rachel's reproving gaze. "Don't say it. I'm micromanaging again."

Dylan put a hand on his shoulder. "None of us would get along without your caretaking," he said. "It's who you are, and Lena will learn to appreciate that." With the other hand, he smothered a yawn. "I've got some work to do before bed, so I'll say good-night. Nice to have you here, Rachel. Come again."

"Thanks, I will."

They watched him disappear into the old barn he'd renovated as a studio and loft.

"I'm glad to hear you'll come back," Garrett said as he and Rachel walked down the hill toward the house and her car. "This wasn't exactly the fun-filled night I promised."

"I had fun. I loved the music." She slanted him a smile. "I even enjoyed the trail mix."

"Me, too." Her hand swung only inches from his, but he wouldn't assume he had the right to take hold of it. "And I appreciated your story. Though I kept waiting for a knight in shining armor to show up. He never did."

"Melody solved her problems on her own. No knight necessary."

He winced. "Ouch. That puts me in my place."

They reached her SUV and Rachel put her hand on the door latch. "I have a question," he said before she could open it.

She looked at him sideways. "Uh-oh."

Pulling in a deep breath, Garrett took the leap he'd been considering all evening. "What did you mean when you said your mom believed in impossibilities?"

RACHEL ATTEMPTED TO divert the question. "I explained, didn't I? Medical school scholarships, for one thing. Boyfriends who weren't jerks. The latest fad diet that promised she could lose weight and never be hungry."

Garrett's intense gaze never left her face. Without a word spoken, she realized he expected more. "But you want the whole truth, don't you?"

"If you'll share."

Maybe it would help him grasp the issue between them. "As I finished medical school, my mother's illness was getting worse. The doctors talked about dialysis, maybe even a kidney transplant. But then my mom discovered this 'healer'—" she drew air quotes around the word "—who promised he could cure her. She wouldn't require dialysis or a transplant, he said, if she put her faith—and her money—in him. Mom mortgaged her house and gave him as much cash as she could raise, believing she would be cured. I was a doctor at this point.

I could have helped her. Instead, she died, still believing this man would make her well."

"That's criminal."

"You're right—and he's in jail for fraud as we speak. But that didn't save my mom."

Garrett's hands closed around hers, his fingers warm against her icy ones. "Did you have family to help you deal with this?"

"It was always just us."

"You've been through a terrible tragedy," he said in a low voice. "I can imagine how that would affect your view of religion and those who have faith. Especially if you had to face that loss on your own."

"Then you see…" She let the words trail off.

He tightened his grip on her hands. "What I see is that you've come to a place where there are people you can depend on. People to care about you and to care for you. God knows, I'm one of them. In the story you told Amber, Melody didn't accomplish her quests on her own. With each trial, she had help—from the birds and the deer, from the river, from the ants. And now you have help. You don't have to stand alone against the world anymore."

She blinked against sudden tears. "I don't understand what you're asking."

"Trust me. Not as a minister or a leader, but as a man. Could you do that?"

Meeting his gaze, she read in his face a yearning she would never have expected, a longing that pierced her defenses. Her confession had created the opposite effect to what she intended.

"I can try," she whispered uncertainly. "I can try."

For a moment, she thought he would take her in his arms, seal their agreement with kisses. She hoped that he would.

But he gave her only a wide smile. "That's wonderful. Thanks." Letting go of her hands, he opened her car door. "And now you'd better get home. Tomorrow is a workday."

Rachel took a deep breath, trying to regain her balance. "It is. And I have patients scheduled." She pulled her keys out of her pocket and sat behind the wheel. "It was a lovely campfire."

Garrett nodded. "We'll do it again. With a better ending."

"I like this ending," she said and started the engine. He was still staring, jaw hanging loose, when she circled onto the driveway and drove off into the dark.

GARRETT CALLED A family meeting at seven on Tuesday morning, since they all happened to be in the kitchen drinking coffee anyway.

"Thomas, Marcos and Lena are bored with the bucking barrel," he announced. "They want to ride live animals."

"Of course they do," Ford said. "That doesn't mean it's a good idea. I'm not sure our insurance will cover that liability."

Caroline sat on a stool at the counter. "Are they ready for live animals?"

Dylan poured himself a second cup. "How do you know until they try?"

"We'd need a chute and a gate," she said. "And steers the right size. Where would we find them?"

Wyatt leaned against the counter. "Dave Hicks on the Twin Oaks Ranch supplies livestock to some of the local shows. He's got an arena set up, and he might have the animals. I can check with him."

"The safety issues worry me." Caroline played with the handle of her mug. "Somebody could get hurt."

"We were planning to let them enter a rodeo at the end of the summer," Garrett reminded her. "They ought to have experience with live animals before then. They'll all be wearing helmets, mouth guards and safety vests. And they've fallen often enough."

"But they've never had to dodge flying hooves," Ford pointed out. "It's a different skill from just falling off the barrel."

"We all rode live animals as kids." Dylan nodded at Garrett. "I don't remember anything but bruises."

"There's always a risk," Ford said.

"Maybe the doctor could come along as medical backup," Wyatt suggested. "If something happens, she'd be right there to take care of it."

"That's an excellent idea," Garrett said. "If she has the time. Her practice is picking up."

Caroline held up her hand. "And what about the four kids who don't want to ride? What would be fun for them to do?"

"They get their own private rodeo," Dylan said. "We could bring snacks, like having a concession stand." Then he frowned. "But I guess food is now a problem, too."

"Dave has a stagecoach and a team of horses." Wyatt went for a refill. "Maybe he could take them on a drive, show them a different part of the country."

"That sounds great." Caroline smiled at him. "Something different for them to do with horses."

"Don't commit to anything until I make sure we're covered." Ford put his mug in the dishwasher. "Right now, I'm going to wake up the boys." He gave Caroline a one-armed hug on his way out the door.

"Is this a go or not?" Garrett asked. "Assuming the insurance allows it."

"I say go." Dylan made a thumbs-up sign. "It'll be an adventure."

Wyatt nodded. "After a summer of barrel practice, I expect they can handle the steers. And the experience will be useful if they enter a rodeo later."

"I guess I'm on board," Caroline said. "Especially if Rachel will come along. That would make me more comfortable." She slipped from her stool and walked over to top up her coffee. "It's time to get the girls up. Catch you all at breakfast."

As she left by the rear door, Dylan stretched his arms wide. "I've gotta wake up. I'm supposed to ride out with Grady at eight to clear that overgrown water ditch in the southeast field. A lovely morning of hacking and digging weeds lies ahead of me. What's on your agenda, Garrett?"

"I'm scheduled for office hours at the church this morning. After the scolding I got Sunday from Ms. Simpson about the time I've been spending with the kids, I figured I'd better show up, even if nobody comes by to check."

First, though, he wanted to talk to Lena. But her team was scheduled to cook breakfast, so he didn't have an opportunity to catch her until after the meal.

"How are you this morning?" he asked, as she brought her plate to the sink to be washed.

She rolled her eyes. "Yes, I tested and did my injection."

He smiled at her. "That's important. But not what I asked."

One thin shoulder lifted in a shrug. "I'm okay, I guess."

Holding open the door to the bunkhouse, Garrett motioned her outside. "You were pretty upset last night."

"Everybody loves s'mores. They were mad when we didn't have them."

"Mad at *you*?" They started up the hill toward the barn.

"That's how it felt. And you didn't trust me not to eat one. Like I'm stupid."

"But you had chips just the night before. How am I supposed to be sure you'll make the best choice?"

Another roll of the eyes. "I'm trying."

"Yes, you are. So am I. And I didn't mean to embarrass you in front of the other kids. I want to trust you, and I want you to be able to trust me."

At the door to the barn, Lena faced him. "Then you should clue me in on what you're planning, so I can decide if I think it's a good idea." Her serious gaze met his. "It's my life."

"Got it." He offered a hand. "I'll consult you before I make any radical decisions about you and food."

She shook with him. "And I'll try not to yell at you in front of people."

That was probably as close as he'd get to an apology. "Deal."

Another parenting lesson. Garrett blew out a deep breath as he walked down the hill toward his truck. *There ought to be a reference book to go by.*

Driving toward town, he realized that the same could be said of women. Especially Rachel Vale. She'd shocked him last night with a simple admission—she'd *liked* how their evening had ended. Meaning, he had to assume, she was glad she'd confided in him. And perhaps she was willing to build a relationship. He'd found it hard to fall asleep, imagining the possibilities now opening up between them.

Of course, her objections to his calling still existed. He understood her reasons now but not how to overcome her resistance. Angry at the con man who had swindled—and effectively murdered—her mother in the guise of religion, Rachel had denied herself the comfort most people found in the community of a church. She was so determined not to be deceived or betrayed that she found it hard to trust anyone.

But she'd said she would try. Garrett only hoped he could prove to her that she'd finally come to a safe place—in this town, with his family and friends, with the people she would come to know as her patients.

And, as he found himself hoping more passionately every day, with him.

Chapter Nine

Tuesday's first-aid session went pretty well, in Rachel's opinion. She covered stings and bites, which gave the teenagers a chance to scare each other with descriptions of insects and snakes, as well as attacks from dogs and wildlife. They discussed the facts about rabies and other diseases carried by animals. To give them something active to do, she brought out various bandages and assigned each kid a different type of wound to be wrapped up. Caroline, Ford and Dylan joined in the laughter at their unskilled efforts.

To her surprise, though, Garrett was nowhere to be seen. Or perhaps the surprise was not that he wasn't there but that she missed him. She'd counted on his assistance with the bandaging project, remembering how his humorous approach always encouraged the kids to have fun. And yet he somehow managed to keep them in line, distracting Marcos from arguing with Thomas, and drawing Lena and Justino's attention away from each other. For her, the experience didn't seem to be as enjoyable without him.

The realization disturbed her as she drove back to the clinic. She had said she'd try to trust him, and she would. But had she already come to depend on him as part of her life here in Bisons Creek? Was he already more than just an acquaintance? More than a *casual* friend?

Fortunately, her afternoon schedule contained enough appointments to keep her from ruminating about Garrett. A construction worker with a bad cut on his palm added excitement to the mix. She reached her last patient of the day about ten minutes behind schedule, and entered the exam room with an apology on her lips.

"You're late." The older woman in the chair glared at her. "My appointment was at four thirty." Tall and somewhat overweight, wearing an unfashionable dress and with her brown hair scraped into a bun, she reminded Rachel of a terrifying algebra teacher she'd had in high school. "I expect you to be prompt." Her voice was low and hoarse.

"I'm sorry, Miss Simpson. An emergency came in." She held out a hand. "I'm Dr. Vale. How do you do?"

The patient sniffed. "It's Ms." Her handshake lacked energy. "Ms. Dorothy Simpson."

"I'll remember. What can I do for you today?"

Ms. Simpson pursed her lips. "My hair is coming out. It's there on my comb every day. And I can see how much thinner it is."

"Can you take your hair down, please?"

Rachel examined Ms. Simpson's head and noted that her long hair did seem sparse, though there was no way to determine how recent the condition might be.

"How are you feeling otherwise?" she asked, unfolding her blood pressure cuff. "Let me put this around your upper arm. Just there." She squeezed the bulb. "How is your appetite?"

"I put on a few pounds, so I've been watching what I eat. But the scale keeps going up. It's very frustrating."

By the end of her exam, Rachel had learned even more

about Ms. Simpson's current condition—how she was tired, even after a night's sleep, and how her knees and her shoulders ached so much some days she could hardly go to work.

"I teach science at the junior high school," she said. "I have to be able to stand during classes. This spring, I seemed to be sitting at my desk most of the day." Her mood had been off, as well. "I don't enjoy life as much as I used to. It's hard to get up in the morning."

The most revealing symptom, though, was a slight enlargement of Ms. Simpson's thyroid gland. "Has a doctor ever told you that your thyroid was enlarged?"

"What does that mean?"

Rachel gave her a reassuring smile. "We're going to run some blood tests to find out."

After taking the sample, Rachel leaned her hips against the counter and folded her arms. "My suspicion, Ms. Simpson, is that you've developed hypothyroidism—your thyroid isn't producing hormones at the right level. If the lab results confirm this, we can start you on a medication to replace those hormones and improve your overall health. We'll find out in just a few days."

"Will my hair grow in again?"

"I can't promise, but it's possible."

"Humph." Ms. Simpson pulled her hair into a ponytail. "I understand you've been occupied with those teenagers the Marshall brothers are so determined to reform. Troublemakers, every last one of them. I've had them all in class and I know."

Rachel tamped down her irritation. "That's the point, isn't it? To redirect their energies and help them imagine a better future for themselves?"

"It's a wasted effort, if you ask me. They'll revert to their old ways as soon as they're home again." She got to her feet. "But then, Pastor Garrett is always trying to rescue somebody. He's a regular down at the shelter in Casper—cooking meals, driving people places, teaching Bible lessons."

"That sounds both helpful and compassionate."

"Except that his church is here, in Bisons Creek. We pay his salary and we should be able to reach him. He's stretched thin enough this summer already, taking on extra ranch work while Wyatt recovers. There was no call to bring in a bunch of hooligans, too."

Annoyance won the upper hand. "Garrett believes it's worth the effort."

"Humph," Ms. Simpson said again. "I didn't notice you in church on Sunday, did I?"

"No, you didn't. If that's all—"

"We'll expect you next week." With her hand on the door knob, she gazed over her shoulder at Rachel. "Going to church matters to people in this town. It means you belong."

When the door shut, Rachel glanced around for something to throw. She'd never had a patient who'd made her this furious. So much for Garrett's assurance that she had come to a place where there were people to depend on. Trusting Ms. Simpson would be similar to trusting a rattlesnake coiled at your feet with his rattles going full speed.

Remembering the encounter over supper at her apartment, she wanted to call Garrett and complain about the terrible Ms. Simpson. Talking to him would soothe her temper and help her put the incident in perspective, but she hated to be a tattletale. And if she didn't want to talk about what had happened this afternoon, her only excuse for calling would be...wanting to hear his voice, to get his perspective on the day. Unwilling to admit such a thing, Rachel jumped up from the table and got to work cleaning the kitchen.

With the dishwasher running and the counters clear, she tuned the radio to a country oldies station and focused her attention on the first-aid lesson for Wednesday, which would be an important one—the Heimlich maneuver for choking and resuscitation for a victim who wasn't breathing. The teenagers wouldn't practice on each other, of course, but she wanted to make them aware of the basics in case they ever faced an emergency.

She finished her planning about nine, stacked her materials and then poured herself a glass of wine to relax with. The radio was playing an hour of "classic country's best love songs." Curled in a corner of the couch, she let the ballads wash over her, mellowing out the irritation she still hadn't quite shaken.

A sudden knock at the front of the house made her jump in alarm. Who would want to visit her after dark? She approached the door with caution, not sure she should open it. At least she hadn't changed into pajamas.

"Rachel, it's Garrett," he said loudly through the open window. "Are you at home?"

Blowing out an exasperated breath, she flipped on the porch light, unhooked the chain, unlatched the dead bolt and turned the doorknob. "Where else would I be at—" she checked her watch "—nine twenty at night?"

"A campfire?" He grinned as he tipped his hat. "Sorry it's so late, but we just finished up at the ranch."

She swung the door open. "Come in."

"Actually, it's really nice tonight. Would you consider coming out?"

An odd request but… "Okay." Stepping onto the porch in her bare feet, she drew a breath of fresh, cool air. "It is a lovely evening. I hadn't been outside since I got home."

Crickets rasped loudly in the darkness, a counterpoint to the music coming through the window.

Garrett leaned his hips against the porch rail and folded his arms over his chest. In the golden glow of the porch lamp, he appeared every inch a cowboy—broad shouldered, slim hipped and totally masculine.

Rachel swallowed hard. "What's the occasion? Is Lena all right?"

"She's fine. I needed to talk to you."

"You, um, could have called." Which would have been less…stimulating.

He shrugged one shoulder. "But I missed visiting with you at lunch. I heard the bandaging session was pretty funny."

She went to stand beside him so she wouldn't stare at him. "Most of the kids ended up mummified. But they at least learned how to tie a sling. And maybe wrap an ankle." The problem with being beside him was the whiff of his scent she caught and the sense of his body so near to hers.

"Lucky for them they live in a town with a great doctor to do the wrapping for them if they get hurt. Speaking of which…" He drew an audible breath. "What's your opinion on rodeos?"

She blinked in surprise at the quick change of subject. "In general? They're fun to watch. I enjoy the barrel racing and calf roping best. Oh, and the clowns. Those guys who ride bulls are insane."

"Ford would disagree."

"He was a bull rider?"

"He was. Dylan went for saddle broncs and I competed bareback. Wyatt was the roper. I guess we were all young and a little crazy."

"Or a lot crazy. Those guys get hurt constantly."

"We four managed to come through without too much damage."

"Lucky you." With no trouble, Rachel could imagine him ten years younger, climbing onto a bronco and getting bucked around. He'd probably grinned during the entire event.

"Yeah. The thing is, the kids have been practicing on the bucking barrel, simulating a rough-stock ride. Now they—Marcos, Thomas and Lena—want to get on a live animal."

"You're considering it?"

"We had talked about letting them enter a junior rodeo at the end of the summer, and they could use some experience before then. Just steers, though. Not bulls. They'll be wearing protective gear."

So he hadn't come because he'd missed her at lunch. He'd come to ask a favor. She ignored her disappointment. "And how am I involved?"

Garrett shifted to face her. "We're hoping you'll come along as our medical support. Just in case."

Rachel raised a skeptical eyebrow. "Just in case. What you ought to have is an ambulance and a couple of EMTs. This camp of yours is getting to be a high-risk enterprise."

"Kids mature through meeting challenges, mental and physical," he said. "When they succeed, their self-image improves. I would say those three kids, in particular, ought to have that kind of reinforcement."

"At the risk of their well-being?"

"Steer riding is pretty tame in comparison to some of the risks they could take in the next few years. Driving under the influence, for example. Carrying a knife, or a gun. Joining a gang."

"Point taken." Shaking her head, she gazed into the

night. "I'm not in Seattle anymore. I guess for people around here, riding steers is a rite of passage."

"For some of them, at least. Lots of kids growing up on ranches start when they're young, riding sheep or calves. It's a Western tradition, after all." Garrett put a hand on her upper arm. "I'm aware this will take you away from your patients. We'll be glad to reimburse you."

"That's not the point," Rachel said sharply, moving out from under his touch. "I can volunteer if I choose. When are you planning to do this?"

"Next week. I can get you the exact date tomorrow."

"That will work." And now that he'd gotten what he came for, he could be on his way and she could resume her evening. Alone. "If that's all..." With her hand on the doorknob, she looked over her shoulder. "I'll let you go."

Garrett shook his head. "No, that was just the hard part. Now we can enjoy ourselves. Will you dance with me?"

"What?" She pivoted to face him.

"The music," he said, with a nod toward the inside of the house where the radio still played. "You've got a nice wide porch here. We could dance."

Rachel gasped a laugh. "You really are crazy." And this was getting out of hand. She should ask him to leave before something happened that she'd regret.

His grin was white in the darkness. "When you live in a small town, you take your opportunities where you find them." He walked over and held out his right hand. "May I?"

At that moment, the opening notes for "Crazy" by Patsy Cline wafted through the window.

Her good sense deserted her. "My all-time favorite." Rachel sighed and put her hand in his. "I can't resist."

His left arm came around her waist. "Lucky me," he murmured, and moved her into the rhythm of the song.

She'd never danced to this number before. For a few moments the blend of words and melody and motion held her in a kind of trance. But then she became aware that it was Garrett's chest against her cheek, his thighs brushing against hers, his breath warm over her ear. In response to his closeness, a shiver ran through her from head to toe.

"Cold?" He drew her closer still, so their bodies touched from her shoulders to her knees.

Gazing up at him, she shook her head. "You're very adept at this."

"Dancing?"

"That, too."

His grin conveyed that he understood her meaning. He was an expert at getting under her guard.

The radio switched to another song and they continued to dance, not just swaying in one place but moving all around the porch as Garrett guided her with smooth steps and sure hands. Rachel relaxed for once, letting go of her defenses and her resistance, allowing herself simply to enjoy the moment. With his arm circling her tightly and his fingers wrapped around hers, she felt *safe*. Loneliness and uncertainty retreated, and she seemed to be protected in a way she'd never experienced in her life.

And if she was safe, then she might be free to follow her instincts, to listen to her own needs and desires. She could hold on to Garrett's broad shoulders with both hands, sensing the power and strength he kept so completely under control. Both his arms were around her now, his hands spread wide at her waist, and she could yield to his gesture, pressing against him as their steps slowed to a standstill.

She could lift her head to meet his gaze as he stared

down at her and then rise up on her toes to press her lips against his.

His mouth was warm and very ready, responding with just the right firmness to assure her she was welcome. He tilted his head, perfecting their fit, and she sighed because she'd been trying so hard not to imagine this and it was more wonderful than it had been in her dreams.

Short and soft. Deep and lingering. The tangle of tongues, the nip of teeth on a lower lip. A slight taste of coffee and the scent of lime on his skin. Absorbed and beguiled, Rachel indulged in the pleasure of kissing Garrett Marshall.

Then her control started to slip. Her breathing came faster. So did his. She wanted—craved—more from him, more of him. His arms banded around her and she linked hers behind his neck, while the kisses got wilder, fiercer, and her body started to ache.

"Come inside," she said as he dragged his lips along her throat. "We can be comfortable."

He went still, though his heart still pounded against hers.

After a motionless moment, she drew back, trying to read his face. "Garrett?"

A shuddering breath lifted his shoulders. "You tempt me," he said, his voice rough. His arms loosened, then let her go altogether. "I'm sorry, Rachel."

"That means no?" She brought her hands to the center of his chest but didn't step away.

"It's a small, rural town. My congregation has certain… expectations…of me. My lifestyle. Spending the night with you—as I'm dying to do—would violate those expectations."

"No one has to know."

"Secrecy doesn't exist in a place like Bisons Creek."

Turning aside, he gripped the top of the porch rail with both hands. "Everybody would find out."

"What happens then? They fire you?"

"It's possible. But much worse would be the disillusionment and loss of faith the members would suffer. As old-fashioned as it might seem, they want their minister to be an honorable man, and their definition of honorable includes no sex without a wedding." He gave a ghost of a laugh. "We could get married."

"Not tonight." Rachel rubbed her temples with her fingers. "That's a very difficult standard to live with."

"Not until right now." He straightened and shoved his hands into his pockets. "I apologize for letting…things… go too far." His smile flashed and was gone. "You're a hard woman to resist."

His boot heels sounded on the floorboards as he crossed the porch. From the bottom of the steps, he looked up at her. "Go on inside. I'll leave when I hear the lock click."

She started to argue that she could take care of herself. But this wasn't a moment for manufactured conflict. There were enough obstacles between them. "Thanks."

Through the window, she watched him walk across the yard to his truck. The lights flashed and then he drove into the night.

Leaning her shoulders against the door panel, Rachel closed her eyes and relived those moments in his arms. Her body still thrummed with unsatisfied desire. And her emotions…

Her emotions were in turmoil. She had let her guard down completely tonight, had been willing to give Garrett anything and everything he asked for. Despite the differences between them, she'd offered herself without reservation.

Only now, in hindsight, did she understand why. It wasn't the music, or the dancing, or even the wine, which sat almost untouched on the table beside the couch. Kissing Garrett had been her choice, made for only one reason.

Despite all her reservations, she was falling in love with him.

GARRETT DIDN'T GO HOME. He couldn't face his brothers, and certainly not Caroline, after what he'd done. Not till he had some kind of control over his guilt.

Instead, he drove to the church and went into his office. Sitting in the desk chair, he propped his elbows on his knees and put his face in his hands. He wanted to hide.

He'd told Rachel his congregation expected their minister to be honorable. Well, he definitely didn't fit that description. An honorable man wouldn't treat a woman the way he'd treated her tonight, wouldn't take advantage of her vulnerability. The fact that she'd kissed him first didn't matter. He should have kept a tight grip on his own response, the hot desire she stirred in him, and gentled the situation. She deserved that kind of respect.

How would he face her when she came to the ranch tomorrow? For that matter, what hope did he have that Rachel would still be willing to pursue a relationship with him? He'd asked her to trust him, but at the first opportunity, he'd broken that trust. Why should she give him another chance?

Somewhere around 2:00 a.m., he managed to ask for forgiveness and accept it. He was human, after all, and mistakes were inevitable. He still wasn't sure how he could make amends or what he could say to restore the balance between Rachel and himself. If she wanted nothing more to do with him, then he would be her *casual* friend and live with it. Somehow.

Sleep, when he finally did go home, was a long while coming.

Rachel avoided him when she arrived the next day at noon. Not obviously, but he couldn't catch her eye. As the kids ate, she stood with Caroline, talking about weddings, and he hesitated to interrupt. Then she started her lesson on the Heimlich maneuver and CPR, too important a subject to joke about. Even the kids seemed to appreciate the seriousness of the content.

While she packed up her materials, he took his chance. "They paid attention," he said, standing on the opposite side of the table. "You made a real impression."

She was still avoiding his gaze. "I appreciated their cooperation."

"They have their angelic moments."

A smile tilted her lips. "Though sometimes that's hard to remember."

"True." He opened the door for her. "We've set up the steer-riding event, by the way. We'll go next Monday, if that works for you."

"I'll clear my schedule," she said, "so I can be free all day." She took an audible breath. "Now, though, I'm due at the office. I have patients this afternoon."

"I'm glad to hear that. I'll walk you to your car."

"No, you don't have to." She put out a hand. "You have other things to do." Finally, her eyes met his, with an expression of near panic.

Garrett stepped away. "Sure." He swallowed hard. "Have a pleasant afternoon."

"You, too." Rachel hurried down the hill on her own.

That was when he was sure he'd ruined his prospects for a life with Rachel Vale.

There was, however, no chance to give in to despair. He found himself even busier than usual that afternoon as he made arrangements for the welcome party on Friday night. Food would be provided by the excellent cooks who resided in Bisons Creek, but there were numerous details for which he was responsible. Tables and chairs, ice, drinks, lights, music... He spent hours on the phone, recruiting volunteers to help provide the essentials.

Thursday morning, he and Lena drove into Buffalo for her doctor's appointment. They had to wait almost two hours past their scheduled time due to an emergency. Garrett discovered that teenagers didn't accept delays with patience, but he acquired some paper from the reception desk and engaged her with tic-tac-toe and hangman, which forestalled most of her complaints.

The doctor, when they saw him, was pleased with her lab results, and the record of her tests and injections over the week. They also talked with Kim Kaiser, the nurse educator, about food choices and their effects on diabetes. Lena was cooperative and polite throughout the meetings, which was more than Garrett had expected. As a reward, he took her to lunch at a diner in Buffalo—she'd brought her backpack containing her test kit and insulin pen, so she didn't have to miss her noon injection.

"You're getting the hang of this," he said when she returned from the restroom. "Congratulations on being prepared."

She rolled her eyes as she sat down across the booth. "Welcome to the rest of my life."

They didn't make it to the ranch for the first-aid session, but they joined in on the fishing trip he and Dylan had put together for the afternoon. They took the kids to a pond in the foothills where the fish practically jumped out of the water to be caught. Lizzie refused to bait the hook and chose to sit under a tree rather than join the rest of the kids by the water. Thomas made the first catch, but Marcos got one of his own soon enough. Within a couple of hours, everybody who wanted one had a fish story to relate at dinner.

And then there was the rest of the evening to get through as if nothing was wrong. He played badminton with the kids and helped churn ice cream, though neither he nor Lena took a serving.

"That leaves more for me," Thomas said, with a greedy laugh.

"And me." Marcos held out his bowl. "You don't get it all."

"Back off," Garrett snapped. "You two aren't the only people who want seconds. Lizzie? Becky? How about another scoop? Justino? Nate?"

He was aware of Ford's sharp eyes on him as he doled out the last of the dessert. Caroline, too, had noticed his irritation. No, he hadn't lost his temper with the kids before. But those two boys had to stop pushing the boundaries. A line should be drawn somewhere.

Leaving the bunkhouse after bed check, he saw Caroline and Ford sitting on the porch of the cabin and gave a sigh of relief. He would get to his room without having to explain or excuse his reaction. Or anything else.

Wrong. As he approached the house, he found Wyatt leaning against a porch post. "A nice night," his brother said, after a nod in greeting. "Fine hay-making weather."

Garrett nodded, relieved at the neutral comment. "The second cutting is coming up strong. We should be able to cut and bale in the next couple of weeks."

"Not if you wear yourself out first."

So much for neutral. He dropped into a rocker. "I'm okay."

"You're tired. And you didn't come in until after two last night. I don't intend to pry—"

"Then don't. I wasn't with Rachel that late, in case you're asking. I went to the church. I had some thinking to do."

"About Rachel." When Garrett didn't answer, Wyatt shook his head. "She's got you twisted up inside."

"It's not her fault. She didn't want me to fall in love with her." There. He'd said it. "In fact, she warned me not to."

"You don't always have control over such things."

"No, you don't."

Wyatt stepped over and put a hand on his shoulder. "I'm sorry. Maybe it'll get easier over time."

"Maybe."

But Garrett wasn't counting on it.

Chapter Ten

Friday was Rachel's first really busy day at the office. Patients started arriving at 8:00 a.m., some without appointments. Allie assured everyone that they would be seen, but fitting them all in before noon was a challenge, and she ended up being late getting to the Circle M for the last first-aid session.

She hurried into the bunkhouse, imagining that the kids would be playing with their phones, waiting on her. But they were all seated at the table and focused on Garrett, who appeared to be in the middle of a story.

"Then this bull wheels around hard to the left, and I completely lose it and fall off. But..." He met each teenager's gaze around the table. "But my hand is stuck. So now I'm hanging from the rope, and that animal is going crazy, trying to get rid of me—bucking, twisting, rearing, anything he can do to dump the stupid cowboy still attached to his shoulders. Meanwhile, I'm pretty sure I'm going to die."

"How did you escape?" Thomas asked, as the others laughed.

"The rigging finally loosened up enough that my hand slipped out. I dropped to the ground facedown, with my arms over my head, just in case. Only when I was sure that bull was shut up in the pens did I get to my feet and leave the arena. And that's my first and only bull ride. I can take a hint." He noticed Rachel then, but his glance didn't linger on her face. "Now here's Dr. Vale to take over. What's on the agenda for your last day?"

"Poisoning," she announced, stepping up to the table. "And shock."

"Important stuff," he told the kids. "There will be a quiz afterward." As they protested, he grinned and shook his head. "I'm kidding. But pay attention anyway." He lifted a hand as he headed for the door.

"I'm sorry I'm late," Rachel said to the teens, pulling her attention away from the man who was leaving. "What kind of substances could be poisonous?"

Another lively discussion ensued, which Rachel wrapped up by reviewing some basic safety considerations—outdoor and sports concerns, and fire prevention, especially. She ended with the question she'd been asking every day. "What's the first thing you do in an emergency?"

"Call 911!" the seven kids yelled.

"Right answer," she said with pride. "Thanks for your attention this week. Stay safe."

To her surprise, they all applauded. "Thank you," Becky said. "We learned a lot."

"I'll keep my book always," Lizzie added. "I might even use it one day."

The boys, of course, didn't volunteer compliments. But Lena came up to her as the meeting broke up. "It must take a lot of studying to be a doctor. Just learning the stuff in that book would take forever. And you probably know so much more."

"About eleven years of work after high school," Rachel said. "You add information piece by piece and it all builds up."

"You have to be pretty old, then," Lena said. "That's a long time."

Caroline, who was listening, started laughing and Rachel joined her. "I've got a few years left."

"It's interesting that Lena asked about medical training," Caroline said as they left the bunkhouse together. "Maybe she'll consider being a doctor or a nurse."

"That would be terrific, wouldn't it? And now's the moment to start." Rachel noticed that Garrett's truck was missing from the collection of vehicles near the house. She wouldn't ask where he might have gone. "I hope these first-aid lessons may have helped to inspire her."

Caroline folded her into a hug. "Thank you so much for doing this. I'm sure it's been a chunk out of your weekdays, but the kids learned in spite of themselves." She stepped away but held on to Rachel by the shoulders. "And we'll meet up with you tonight at the party. From all the planning Garrett's been doing, it should be really fun!"

The idea of Garrett organizing the party stayed with Rachel during the afternoon, sneaking into her mind in those moments when she wasn't focusing on medicine. It was typical of him to make an extra effort, to take on more than his share of what could have been a simple coffee-and-soft-drinks affair. His dedication to the projects he adopted—the kids' camp, or Lena's care, let alone a welcome party—was compelling.

As if she wasn't already smitten enough. She could hardly speak to him without revealing the state of her emotions. Facing him tonight at the party would take a level of courage she wasn't sure she possessed. With the whole town watching, she would have to treat Garrett as if he was a casual friend and nothing more.

Which was funny, because that was all she'd wanted

in the first place. Falling in love with Garrett Marshall was absolutely the last thing she'd intended to do. And yet somehow, in just a few days, he'd come to matter to her as no man ever had. He made her laugh and he made her think. He made her want a kind of relationship she'd never experienced—the trusting, committed, enduring bond between husband and wife.

After work, as she dressed for the party, Rachel admitted to herself that what she wanted couldn't happen, for reasons she'd recognized from the first day they met. She would make Garrett unhappy. He required a wife who would be a part of the church—a role she couldn't fill.

In fact, the pain she'd predicted had already arrived. She walked toward Hayley Brewster's house, carrying the certainty that any connection with Garrett wouldn't last. Nothing about their situation had changed, except her feelings for him. Rachel could only hope that the ache in her heart would fade eventually.

She heard music at about the same moment she noticed the parked cars and trucks lining the curb on both sides of the street. Up ahead was her destination, a big Victorian house with a wraparound porch, which tonight was draped with strings of white lights. More lights had been strung around the edges of the yard, creating a carnival atmosphere enhanced by the five-piece band on the side porch playing mellow country music. Men in Western hats chatted with women in boots and jeans, while children of various sizes and ages chased each other around and through the shifting groups of adults. There was even a group of teenagers, gathered in a clump just as the kids at the ranch often did, staring at their phones.

Standing across the street, Rachel swallowed hard. They all seemed acquainted, and the prospect of wading into the crowd on her own suddenly daunted her. If she could find one person she'd met…

"If it isn't the guest of honor." All at once, Garrett stood beside her, smiling. "Want some reinforcements?"

Her heart started to race. Then she noticed his brothers and Caroline right behind him, plus Susannah, Amber and all seven teenagers. "You brought the whole crew!" Their presence eased her nerves. Having the whole Marshall crowd to depend on somehow made her less vulnerable.

"The better to welcome you." He gestured for her to move forward. "Let's go initiate some introductions."

In fact, Hayley Brewster was the first person they encountered as they stepped onto the grass. "There you are," she said, taking Rachel by the arm. "Everybody's waiting to meet you. You'd better get some food first, though, so you'll have your strength."

Hayley guided her to a line of tables set up along one side of the space, their surfaces covered with pots, pans and casserole dishes. As the first in line, Rachel had her choice of all the wonderful food but could hardly make a decision between one home-cooked dish and the next.

"That's my chicken and dumplings," the woman behind her said, pointing to a red kettle. "My grandmother's recipe. I'm Beverly Long, by the way." She offered a handshake. "Welcome to Bisons Creek. What should I take for my arthritis?"

"I'll be glad to talk to you about that." Rachel scooped up the chicken and dumplings. "Just call the office and let Allie make you an appointment."

Minutes later, as she stood eating with Ford and Garrett, an older gentleman in a tall hat and a bolo tie approached. "I'm Paul Morris, Dr. Vale. I had pneumonia last winter and was just coughing my lungs out. I had to keep driving to Buffalo to visit the doctor—a real ordeal, especially with all the snow we had. I'm real glad that I don't have to go so far for help these days."

She swallowed a bite of potato casserole while shaking his hand. "And I'm glad you're looking so well, Mr. Morris. We'll do our best to keep you that way."

"Let me take your plate," Ford said, glancing around. "You're about to get very busy."

Gallstones, psoriasis, allergies and indigestion—Rachel heard about all of them and more as she greeted the citizens of Bisons Creek. For every person who just wanted to say hello, there was someone else with symptoms to report.

"Does this always happen?" Garrett asked after one particularly detailed recital.

"People are concerned about their health," she told him. "It's a point of connection between us."

He tilted his head. "Come to think of it, I guess ministers have their own version of that pattern. The moment you meet someone, they want to discuss theology so you can confirm their beliefs and assuage their doubts. Or else they're hoping for a counseling session."

"Occupational hazards," Rachel said.

"And you said we don't have anything in common."

Her cheeks grew warm. "I might have been wrong about that."

His serious gaze held hers and he took a step closer. "I'm listening."

At that moment, a tap on the shoulder snared her attention. "Don't monopolize the lady, son." Flustered, Rachel found herself confronted by a large man in a Western-cut blue suit. "Dr. Vale, I'm Herbert Jolly, mayor of this fine town." He gave her hand a bruising shake. "I apologize for not being here to greet you before this—I was in Las Vegas at a conference all week long. But we are delighted to have you hang out your shingle in our neck of the woods. Anything I personally can do to make things easier for you, just call my office. I answer the phone myself."

"Because his office is his kitchen table," Garrett said over her shoulder as the mayor moved off to speak with Hayley Brewster. "At least he didn't share the details of the kidney stone he passed last fall. It's a long, painful story."

Laughing, she shook her head. "I'm sure." Her attention was claimed by someone else and when she got free again, Garrett had moved to the far side of the yard, where he stood talking with two young, pretty women she hadn't yet met. Members of his congregation, she guessed. The type who would adore being a pastor's wife.

Jaw clenched, Rachel sent her gaze in a different direction and caught sight of the kids from the ranch camp, seated together on the steps of the porch. At the other end of the front walk stood the teenagers she'd noticed earlier with their phones. Something about the attitudes of the two groups, an aura of antagonism, alerted her. She moved closer to investigate.

"Losers." The word came from the group on the sidewalk. "What are they doin' here anyway?"

"Wastin' space," somebody said, and they all laughed. "Same as in school."

On the steps, Marcos scowled, while Thomas sat with his hands clenched on his thighs. Lena leaned in between them, talking fast.

"Going to summer camp like little kids," came the comment. "And they suckered a bunch of rich people into paying for it."

Thomas stood up, but Lizzie grabbed his hand and pulled him back down on the step.

"Those Marshalls are pretty stupid, trying to make a difference with gangbangers and lowlifes. Why not spend their money on kids who deserve it?"

Both now on their feet, Marcos and Thomas strode toward the group, fists swinging at their sides.

Rachel stepped toward them, reaching out.

A hand closed around her arm, restraining her. "No," Garrett said.

She glanced at him in alarm. "They're going to fight!"

"And you can't be involved. We'll handle it." She saw that Ford and Dylan had come to stand nearby.

About a foot away from their adversaries, though, the two boys stopped. "The Marshalls are not stupid," Marcos said to the leader, who was shorter by six inches. He stared at the boy for a long, contemptuous minute. "I could destroy you. But you're not worth the effort."

Without another word, he returned to the porch, Thomas at his side. As a group, the seven ranch kids then descended on the dessert table, filled their plates and relocated to the far corner of the yard.

Rachel slumped in relief. "Amazing!"

GARRETT FIGURED HE probably looked like a clown, his grin was so wide. "Can you believe that? They walked away!" The assembly of problem kids dissolved as each of them headed in the general direction of their parents, probably hoping the party would end soon.

"Your optimism paid off," Rachel agreed as they watched the crowd. "Marcos and Thomas chose to avoid a fight."

"It was really a team effort. None of our kids wanted to give in to the provocation. I'm proud of all of them."

"Me, too." She smiled at him, and for a second the noise and the bustle around them faded away, so there was only the two of them, connecting. He wondered if he'd been wrong, if maybe he hadn't ruined everything on Tuesday night...

Then, in the next moment, Dorothy Simpson stood beside them. "Pastor." She gave him a nod. "Dr. Vale, I wanted to add my welcome to those you've already received."

Rachel shook her hand. "Thank you, Ms. Simpson. It's been a wonderful evening. I've enjoyed meeting so many of Bisons Creek's residents."

"Some of whom should have been left at home." Dorothy narrowed her eyes. "It would have been a shame to witness a brawl on Haley Brewster's front walk, Pastor."

Garrett nodded. "Our kids made sure that didn't happen, though I admit they seemed to be sorely tempted."

"Yes, well." She cleared her throat. "I mentioned to Dr. Vale earlier this week that she should make a point of attending services on Sunday. Church membership is an important means of becoming part of the community. Don't you agree?"

He swallowed his surge of anger. "That's one way, certainly. But far from the only one. I expect Rachel will become part of the Bisons Creek family because of the care she'll provide, the concern she demonstrates for her patients and her remarkable character."

Dorothy's ample bosom lifted on a deep breath. "You don't encourage church attendance?"

"Of course I do. I've invited Rachel to attend our church. But whether she comes or not is a matter of personal conscience, which she's free to decide for herself."

As Dorothy stalked away in a huff, Rachel gazed at him. "Thanks for the defense."

"My pleasure. Don't let her bully you—she tries it with everyone. I'm always hearing about something new I've done wrong."

There was a question in her eyes, but before he could investigate, Jim and Martha Bolan joined them.

"We were just talking," Jim said, after Garrett had introduced Rachel, "and realized it's been months since we had you over to Sunday dinner, Pastor. And we're correcting that mistake right now by asking you to eat with us this Sunday, right after church. Dr. Vale, we'd love it if you could come, too. Our kids will be there—we've got five of them, all living close, though they couldn't make it tonight—so you'll be able to meet everyone. Don't disappoint us, now. It's the Fair Fields Ranch, on down the road from the Circle M. Pastor Garrett knows how to get there, so maybe you two could ride together."

"I'm making pot roast," Martha added. "Best in the county, Jim says."

"You do have to wonder," Garrett said, as the Bolans left, "how many different pot roasts he's tasted to be certain that hers is the best in the county."

Rachel surveyed the party, which was winding down. "If you have a lot of potluck dinners, he might have been able to sample quite a few."

"Point taken. The church does this kind of thing pretty often. People enjoy eating together."

She gave him a sharp glance. "These sorts of experiences make you a part of the community, right?"

Laughing, he held up his hands in surrender. "I plead the Fifth."

Haley Brewster put a hand on his shoulder. "I'm glad those kids of yours had their wits about them, Pastor. I didn't plan on a rumble at this shindig." She nodded to Rachel. "I believe you're officially off duty, Doc. About the only folks left are the Marshalls and their bunch. You must be tired from shaking so many hands. I sure am."

"Let me help you clean up," Rachel said. "There's a lot to put away."

But Haley wouldn't hear of it. "The Marshalls will deal with it tomorrow. You just get on home." She waved off Rachel's thanks, walked up the porch steps and went into the house.

"She wants a cigarette," Garrett said. "But she hates smoking in front of people."

Rachel frowned. "I suggested she quit."

"Lots of people have, for about sixty years. Including her husband. And he died first, so you probably won't get her to change." Across the yard, he caught a signal from Ford that they were heading for the cars. Steeling his nerve, he put a hand on Rachel's arm. "I've got my truck here. Can I give you a ride home?"

To his surprise, she smiled. "I'd like that."

The walk to his truck took five minutes, and the drive to her place five more. They didn't speak until they started up the sidewalk. "By my estimation, you met most of the town," Garrett said. "I suspect you'll be seeing all of them in your office eventually. You made a great impression." He cleared his throat. "I didn't get a chance to mention earlier how beautiful you are tonight."

She climbed the porch steps and turned to face him. "And I haven't had the opportunity to thank you for organizing the whole event. Caroline mentioned how hard you worked on this evening."

"Just a few phone calls."

"Right." Her hands came to rest on his shoulders. "You're a very generous man, Garrett Marshall. With your time, your attention, your energy."

He pretended to duck his head. The embarrassment, though, was real. "Aw, shucks, ma'am."

When he looked up again, her smile had faded. "So were you just trying to annoy Dorothy Simpson tonight, or did you mean what you said? About whether or not I come to church?"

That searching expression was in her eyes again. Garrett took a deep breath. "I understand your point of view, Rachel. I'm hoping one day you'll change your mind, but until that happens, I can't force you into anything. I won't try."

"Does it bother you? That I don't participate in the community that way?"

He wished she hadn't asked that particular question. "Honestly? Yes."

"Why?" She let her hands drop to her sides.

"I've experienced how rewarding and healing life can be as part of the church. Support in your grief, celebration with your joy—I want those experiences for you as a person I care about."

"But you're willing to accept my choice?"

Garrett tried to lighten the moment. "I'm prepared to tolerate some uncertainty in life. I—"

"Tolerate?" Rachel glared at him. "You're going to *tolerate* me?"

"That's not what I meant." He reached out, but she retreated toward the door. "I should have said *accept*. I *accept* some uncertainty."

She shook her head. "It occurs to me that you're the one who has problems with trust."

"I would trust you with my life. Literally."

But the damage was done.

"This is exactly what I predicted from the very beginning," she said. "We can't have a relationship because we are destined to hurt each other. No matter how we much we lo—care, this one issue will cause conflict until I give in or you give up. How can we be happy under those conditions?"

"I'm willing to try." Even as he said it, he realized he'd lost the battle.

"We shouldn't have to try, Garrett. Being together should be easy and fun. Not something we have to work to get through."

"We get along fine. Rachel—"

"Let's agree to keep our distance," she said, staring somewhere over his shoulder. "That will make things easier."

"We're supposed to have lunch with the Bolans on Sunday. Monday the kids are riding steers. You're the doctor, I'm the pastor. In a town this small—"

"So we'll just…cope." She went the rest of the way to the door. "Good night."

Before he could protest, she'd let herself inside and closed the panel. The click of the lock sounded loud in the darkness.

RACHEL WALKED OUT of the house at twelve thirty on Sunday with her car keys in her hand. Just as she set foot on the sidewalk, Garrett's truck pulled up at the curb. He was already at the passenger door when she got to the curb.

She frowned at him. "What are you doing here?"

"We said I'd pick you up, since I'm familiar with Fair Fields Ranch." He wore his clerical shirt and collar, along with a serious expression she wasn't used to. "There's no sense wasting fuel." He opened the truck door. "Ready to go?"

Short of an undignified argument, there was no way to refuse. "Thanks."

The silence, as they drove out of town, was nerve-racking. "What did the kids do yesterday?" she asked, deciding polite conversation would have to be better. "Bucking practice?"

Garrett nodded. "In the afternoon. Saturday mornings are scheduled for cleanup, when everybody shares in the housework. There's also laundry—all the bedding gets washed."

"I'm sure this happens without complaints."

He glanced at her sideways but didn't smile. "Have you met Marcos? Sure, there are protests, but nothing else happens until the work is done. Boredom will get to them, if peer pressure doesn't." They passed the gate for the Circle M. "We had a campfire Saturday night... with s'mores. Lena settled for trail mix and everyone else was satisfied."

"Good for her. She's come a long way in just a few days."

"She has."

That disturbing silence fell again, and Rachel couldn't conceive of how to break it. She wasn't used to Garrett being quiet. He always seemed to have something to say, usually something funny. But then, nothing seemed especially funny today.

Finally, they came to a set of log gates with ranch buildings visible beyond. "Fair Fields Ranch," Garrett said. "Home of the Bolan clan."

The number of cars parked near the house surprised Rachel, but she was even more startled by the horde of young children running around. "They have grandchildren, too?"

"Twelve or thirteen," he said. "There may be a new one this summer, I can't remember."

And they had all come for lunch. The meal was served buffet-style from the long kitchen counter, with adults seated in the dining room while the older children ate in the breakfast nook. Infants and toddlers joined their parents, which made the atmosphere hectic, to say the least. Keeping track of names proved impossible. There were several juniors among the little boys, plus Junior, the Bolans' oldest son. A gaggle of little girls all seemed to have names starting with *A*—Ashten, Amanda, Avery and Addy among them, but they were so close in age and moved so quickly that Rachel couldn't tell them apart.

At Mrs. Bolan's direction, she and Garrett sat next to each other, which diminished Rachel's appetite considerably. On her other side was a Bolan daughter—Ginny? Jeannie?—with a two-month-old in her arms and a two-year-old in the high chair beside her. Their opportunities for adult conversation were scarce.

As Rachel toyed with her food, Garrett said in a low voice, "Best pot roast in the county. Better eat up."

"You're incorrigible," she said, biting her lip.

His gaze met hers for the first time that day. "At least I can still make you smile."

Though the meal continued for quite a while, she couldn't force herself to eat another bite. He could still make her smile because she loved him, but her awareness of the barriers between them cramped her heart.

"Now, you two be sure to come again," Martha Bolan said as they were leaving. "You'll have noticed how much we enjoy young people." She held Rachel back as her husband walked toward the truck with Garrett. "And I always have a soft spot in my heart for a courting couple."

"Oh...no." Rachel shook her head. "We're not... together. Really."

The older woman winked at her. "I see what I see."

"You could have warned me," Rachel told Garrett when they were in the truck again and outside the Fair Fields gate. "I had no idea there would be so many of them."

"Nothing can prepare you for Sunday lunch with the Bolans," he said. "Actually, the kids were pretty calm today. Imagine their house at Christmas."

"I'd rather not. But her pot roast really is delicious."

"Yes, it is." He grinned at her, she grinned in response, and for a moment there were no barriers, no insoluble conflicts to face. Just the two of them sharing a joke on a sunny Sunday afternoon.

Until Garrett remembered. His grin faded away. He faced forward again, his expression carefully blank.

Embarrassed, Rachel gazed out the side window and surrendered to the silence.

She spoke only when he'd stopped in front of her house. "Thank you for the ride. Lunch was...an experience." When Garrett started to get out, she put up a hand. "I can get it. I'd rather. Really."

"Okay."

She stepped down from the truck and went to close the door, but stood staring, instead, at the pain on Garrett's face.

"Are you sure?" he asked in a rough voice.

Unable to summon her voice, she nodded.

Then she shut the door between them and started down the sidewalk. By the time she'd made it to the steps, he'd driven away and she was free—free to relax, to sit on the top step and put her arms around her bent legs.

Free to put her head down on her knees and let the tears come.

Chapter Eleven

When Garrett entered the bunkhouse on Monday morning, he found two of the boys already awake.

"This will be so cool." Sitting on the arm of the sofa, Thomas had one arm stretched over his head while the other hand grabbed the upholstery. "I'm gonna stick with that sucker no matter which way he goes." Jerking from side to side, he was obviously pretending to ride a bucking animal.

"Yeah, sure." Sprawled in an armchair, Marcos was already dressed. "We'll see who lasts the longest. I'm betting it won't be you."

Thomas stopped riding. "What do you want to bet?"

Marcos rolled his eyes. "You don't have anything I want, dude."

"You're just afraid you're gonna lose."

"I'm not afraid." Marcos surged to his feet, fists clenched. "I will win."

"There's no winning or losing today." Garrett put his hand on Marcos's shoulder. "Just having fun. Do you two have your safety gear ready to go?"

With the conflict averted, he went in to wake Justino and Nate, an easier task than usual because all the kids were excited about the day's adventure at Twin Oaks Ranch. Thomas and Marcos could hardly concentrate on cooking breakfast—the scrambled eggs were a little too well-done and some of the bacon had a bit of char on it. Becky's potatoes were nicely crisp, but Justino had burned the toast.

Garrett surveyed his plate and then quietly dropped the food into the trash while the kids weren't looking.

"Not smart," Ford said quietly. "You're going to wish you had those calories before lunchtime rolls around."

"Coffee's enough." Garrett took a deep draw from his mug. "I'll be okay."

"Considering what little you've eaten in the past few days, I'm not so sure. If you're sick—"

"I'm as healthy as a horse. You worry too much."

"And you're not sleeping enough. I hear you walking around in the middle of the night. What's the problem?"

"Nosy brothers. I'm fine, Ford. Drop it." He emphasized the last two words with a glare.

Ford took offense, as Garrett had hoped he would. "Be glad to." Shoulders stiff, he went to talk to Caroline as she supervised kitchen cleanup.

Making Ford mad was often the only way to distract him. Garrett hated the necessity, but he didn't intend to discuss Rachel with anybody, not yet. Maybe after a while, when the ache had eased, he'd be able to talk about it.

Right now, he was gathering all his strength to face her again. Yesterday's lunch with the Bolans had stretched the limits of his fortitude. Today, at least, he would have the kids demanding his attention, and a crowd of adults to distract him. This trip would not be easy, but somehow he'd have to get through it.

As soon as Caroline approved the kitchen cleanup, they started loading gear into the van—not a moment too soon, as far as the kids were concerned. Susannah brought out boxes of snacks and bagged lunches while Dylan and Garrett lugged coolers full of ice and bottled water. Rachel arrived in the midst of the process, bringing along the giant duffel with all her medical supplies.

Garrett went to meet her. "I'll put that in the truck." He managed a grin. "Thanks for coming along. With luck, your presence will be completely unnecessary."

Her smile was as strained as his. "That's what I'm hoping." She watched the teenagers as they milled around, anxious to get going. "Does Lena have her supplies? And a snack, in case her blood sugar gets low?"

"We've got plenty of food. I checked with her and she says she's brought everything she needs, so we're ready to go. You can ride in the truck or in the van with the kids. Your choice." He wasn't sure which would be easier for him. She would be on his mind either way.

"I'll go with the kids," Rachel said. "In case there's bloodshed."

"Smart plan. Ford and Caroline will be with you." They stood side by side, not speaking, as the kids climbed into the vehicle. Garrett had never felt so awkward, so self-conscious. So hopeless. "We'll meet you at Twin Oaks."

They drove north to Buffalo, then east toward Gillette before heading south into the area bordering the Thunder Basin National Grasslands.

"Such a different landscape." Susannah spoke from the backseat. "Just the rolling prairie and no mountains in sight."

Dylan was riding shotgun. "Now imagine these endless plains being home to huge herds of buffalo. Has Amber ever seen a buffalo?"

"They had one at a rodeo we went to, but she was probably too young to remember."

"Dave Hicks has a small herd at the ranch," Wyatt said from behind Garrett. "You might be able to get a glimpse of them when you're on the stagecoach ride."

"I learned 'bout buffalo," Amber said. "Wyatt read me a story."

Dylan looked at her. "What did you learn?"

"They were stinked," she announced.

There was a moment of silence as the adults sought to understand.

Then Wyatt chuckled. "*Ex*tinct," he said. "The buffalo were almost extinct."

"That's what I said."

Laughing, Garrett followed the van underneath the archway announcing Twin Oaks Ranch. Fences stretching as far as the horizon enclosed rolling pastures dotted with cattle. The white-trimmed brick house sat on a slight rise, with the rest of the ranch complex sprawling around it—barns and work sheds, corrals and pens. Ford stopped the van near a big gray barn and Garrett pulled the truck up beside it. As they all climbed out of the vehicles, a man came striding toward them from a building across the road. He was tall and husky, with red hair and a thick mustache.

"This must be the traveling rodeo show." His voice carried easily to every ear within five hundred feet. "Welcome to the Twin Oaks." He shook Wyatt's hand. "I'm glad you're out and about, man. Had the same thing happen once—seemed I'd never get back to work. Whole place went to hell."

"Lucky for me I've got three brothers to make sure that doesn't happen." Wyatt introduced the adults and then gestured to the kids, standing in a bunch nearby. "And these are your contenders for the day."

Dave Hicks shook hands with each of them. "I'm

happy to have you here. We've got your steers waiting for you in the pen, a stopwatch in my pocket and I'm wearing my whistle 'round my neck." He demonstrated with a quick toot. "Get your gear and let's go scope out the arena."

Marcos, Lena and Thomas rushed to the rear of the van, and then followed the rest of the group in Dave's footsteps as he headed around the side of the barn. In the near distance stood a large metal pen about two hundred feet across, with a bucking chute and a couple of pens on one side. Six steers occupied one of the enclosures, projecting the essence of bovine complacency.

"They don't appear wild," Rachel said, stopping to observe. She'd insisted on carrying her medical duffel herself.

"Right now, they wouldn't waste the energy." Garrett paused beside her. "But put a rider on them, and they suddenly have a mission in life."

"Which is what we're here to do." Shaking her head, she walked on. "I watched some steer-riding videos on the internet. I was not reassured."

He allowed her to walk ahead of him rather than endure the tension between them. When he caught up with the group, Dave was demonstrating the gate in the bucking chute for the kids.

"You'll sit down, wrap your rope good and tight, and then when you're ready, we'll swing this gate open and out you'll go. We've got a nice soft dirt floor for your falling pleasure, so once you've done your eight seconds, just get yourself off."

"When can we ride?" Lena asked, her eyes eager.

Dave laughed at her enthusiasm. "I'll call some extra hands over here and we'll get you started, little lady."

Garrett went to stand by the two boys. "You guys set?"

"Oh, yeah," Thomas said. "This will be so awesome."

Marcos pumped his fist in the air. "I'm riding to the whistle!"

"Not without your vest and helmet," Garrett reminded them. "Better get those on."

The four kids who weren't riding, along with Caroline, Rachel, Susannah and Amber, had settled on a small stand of bleachers placed outside the arena fence. Snacks had been distributed and everybody seemed to be enjoying the morning. Wyatt stood near the chute, and even from a distance Garrett could sense his yearning to be a part of the action instead of a spectator. The summer's forced vacation had been hard on his spirit.

Dave brought three cowboys over to the chute. "These are some real experienced bull riders," he said. "Fred, Steve and Tad. Along with Ford, they're gonna get you situated for each round. Guys, this is Lena, Marcos and Thomas. They'll be riding our steers today." He eyed the youngsters. "So who's first up?"

All three of them raised their hands. Dave gave a big laugh. "Got us three go-getters, here. Thomas, you're looking fierce this morning. We'll let you take the first shot."

Marcos groaned in protest. Garrett put a hand on his shoulder. "You'll get your chance. It never hurts to watch the others. You two go stand behind the fence."

The first steer moved into the chute from the pen and stood quietly enough while Thomas sat down. Ford had promised he'd make sure the kids took a good grip and had the rope wrapped tightly around their gloved hand before he let them go. Tad and Steve climbed down to operate the gate while Garrett and Dylan positioned themselves on either side of the chute. Like rodeo clowns, their role was to help the rider get off as safely as possible.

"Everybody set?" Ford called. Then he asked Thomas, "Ready?"

The boy nodded.

"Go!"

The gate swung open and the steer charged into the arena, bucking hard. Holding on with both hands, Thomas jerked forward, back, forward, back, and then tipped over the right side. Garrett closed in to be sure that the rigging had come loose, as it was supposed to, allowing the boy to fall clear. He landed facedown but quickly scrambled to his feet in the way they'd instructed him, ready to run if the steer came after him. Dylan moved in front of the animal, waving his hat, and it veered off to the left, where Dave held open a gate leading into the pen.

Garrett walked with Thomas to the fence. "You okay?"

"Yeah." He took off his helmet. "I lost my balance."

"You made a decent start. Keep that chest forward and over the shoulders. Did you have fun?"

The boy's dirty face split into a wide grin. "Oh, yeah."

"That's what counts. Go get a snack and a drink." Over at the bleachers, Thomas received a hero's welcome from the spectators, which was probably almost as satisfying as staying on till the whistle.

In the meantime, Marcos had climbed into the chute and was settling on his steer. When Ford yelled, "Go," the steer roared out of the gate, bell clanking, and went into a spin. After just two bucking turns, Marcos dived to the outside, landing on his hands and knees. He was slow to stand, though, and the steer rounded on him, bent on revenge.

Yelling, "Get up!" Garrett jumped between them, flapping the red bandanna he'd brought for the purpose while Dylan came in from the side. Together, they distracted the animal and sent it toward the exit gate. With the coast clear, Garrett spun around, checking for Marcos, but the boy had disappeared.

Retracing their walk from the barn, Garrett found him at the van, sitting inside with his vest and helmet stuffed in his bag. "I'm ready to go," he announced.

"Why the hurry?"

Marcos crossed his arms over his chest. "This is boring."

Garrett clicked his tongue. "One thing I've never heard about rough-stock riding is that it's boring."

After a pause, Marcos said, "I didn't make the whistle."

"Most people don't on their first ride."

"It's nothing like the bucking barrel."

"No, it's not. But the only way to get better is to keep trying. If that's what you want."

"I'm not sure." He was quiet for a minute. "They're bigger than I expected they would be."

Garrett nodded. "The next ride will be better because you'll be more prepared. Whether you make it or not is up to you." Out of the corner of his eye, he noticed someone rounding the corner of the barn, headed toward them. His chest tightened when he recognized Rachel.

"I wondered if Marcos is okay," she said when she reached them. "Is there anything I can do?"

The boy sent Garrett a pleading look.

"He's fine." With a hand on her shoulder, he steered her in the direction she'd just come, walking with her. "Just reviewing his ride."

"I...understand."

From her tone of voice, he realized she probably did. "We're okay so far, at least," he said. "Now we'll find out what Lena can do."

Rachel flashed him an angry glance. "You make it

sound as if she's coming up to bat in a softball game. What she's doing is *dangerous*." Before he could answer, she picked up her speed, walking away from him for the second time that day.

Another female gave him hell when he reached the arena. "Where have you been?" Lena glared at him from her perch on the fence rails. "I'm ready to ride!"

"Go for it," he told her, with Rachel's accusation still ringing in his ears.

Inside the arena, he stood with Dylan while Lena climbed into the chute. "She's a little thing," his brother said. "Seems kinda breakable."

"But she's strong." Garrett needed the encouragement himself. "And she's the best rider we have, except for Nate." Of course, even experienced riders could get hurt.

"Everybody set?" Ford yelled. "Ready, Lena?"

Garrett took a deep breath.

"Go!"

Rearing and bucking, the animal danced across the dirt, jerking Lena forward and back, a rag doll tied to the top of that big old steer. But with her chin tucked, she kept her seat glued to the animal's spine, her legs long on his sides. As the ride went on, she acquired more control, deliberately moving with the motion instead of simply reacting to it. Dave blew the whistle while Garrett was still waiting for her to fall off.

With the instincts of a seasoned cowboy, Lena loosened her grip, threw her leg over and slid to the ground, landing on her feet and then hustling out of the way.

Cheers erupted from the spectators and the men in the chute. Garrett made sure the steer had reached the exit before approaching the grinning girl. "Fantastic!" he yelled, slapping her hands as she held them over her head. "Way to go!"

"I said I could." She spun around and waved her arms at the kids still applauding from the bleachers. "I can do anything!"

A snack break followed, during which Thomas and Marcos sat with their shoulders hunched, frowning, while everyone else celebrated.

When Garrett went to the cooler for a second bottle of water, he turned to find Rachel standing behind him.

"I'm sorry I yelled at you," she said, not quite meeting his eyes. "And I concede your point. Lena just got a tremendous boost of self-confidence."

"That's the value of taking risks. Yes, you might get hurt." Despite his noble intentions, he couldn't help brushing up a strand of hair that had fallen over her forehead. "But you often emerge from the experience stronger and more powerful."

RACHEL UNDERSTOOD. He wasn't talking about the kids. He was talking about her.

She drew a deep breath, but before she could say anything, Lena accosted them.

"Do we get another ride? There were six steers. Can we go again?"

"That's the plan." His quick smile at Rachel was apologetic. Then his attention returned to Lena. "Are you ready?"

"Definitely!"

Rachel sat with Caroline and Susannah on the bleachers. "Three more rides," she told them. "One each." Blowing out a breath, she prepared to wait it out.

Lena, emboldened by her success, wanted to go first. But when her steer went into a spin, she fell off a couple of seconds before the whistle. Whatever Garrett said in consolation didn't have much effect, and she came out to sit with Lizzie and Becky still pouting.

Thomas made a much better show on his next ride, staying on for almost the full eight seconds. He left the arena shaking his head, but bragged to Justino, "Next time, I'll make it."

That left Marcos. Rachel gathered he'd suffered a crisis of confidence after falling off on his first ride, but had chosen to go again. And his determination paid off—though he was jerked around in every possible direction, he somehow managed to stay on top until the whistle blew.

Then Caroline gasped. "He's stuck."

Marcos was hanging by one arm from the rope wrapped around the steer. Still anxious to be rid of its rider, the animal dragged him from one side of the arena to the other. Garrett and Dylan closed in, trying to release the boy. Endless moments passed.

Suddenly, Marcos dropped to the ground. The rope fell off. Garrett and Dylan drove the steer away from the boy lying in the dirt.

Rachel started running.

Before she reached him, though, he was on his feet. "I'm okay," he said, grinning widely. "My foot got stepped on. My hand hurts. But I made the whistle!" He limped out of the arena to the viewing stand.

She cornered him there. "Let me examine your hand. Can you move your fingers?" Though his palm was swollen and red from being caught in the rope, there didn't seem to be obvious damage. His foot was bruised but otherwise fine. "You're lucky," she informed him, handing over his glove. "I hope you're aware of that."

As happy as she'd ever seen him, Marcos only shrugged. "I made the whistle."

Rachel glanced in frustration at Garrett, standing nearby.

Hands in his pockets, he shrugged. "Sometimes you get hurt, but you win anyway."

His comment did not improve her frame of mind. He was implying that taking the risk of a relationship might get them hurt, but they would emerge stronger and happier for the experience.

She wasn't convinced.

After lunch, Dave Hicks led them to the horse barn where he kept his stagecoach. The teenagers observed with fascination as four horses were harnessed to the vehicle, while Dave explained the history of travel in the old West. A ride around the ranch provided the kids with a view of the bison herd and the gorgeous grasslands of the area.

Their return to the barn signaled the end of the adventure. Dave accepted their heartfelt thanks and made sure to speak with Lena, Marcos and Thomas individually.

"All three of you did a great job," he said. "Just getting on the steer makes you a winner."

From the size of their grins, they believed him.

The excitement of the day proved to be a potent sedative—every one of the kids was asleep before they had traveled half an hour. Caroline had insisted on sitting in the second seat, and even she dozed off, with Becky's head on her shoulder.

Rachel sat in the front with Ford, who was driving. "Today has been quite an undertaking," she volunteered, since it would be rude to say nothing the entire trip. "All the kids really enjoyed themselves."

"Dave made a big effort on our behalf. But that's the way he does everything—one hundred and ten percent.

We'll have everybody write him thank-you notes tomorrow." He grinned. "They'll love that."

"But so will he, I imagine. Letter writing is a lost art." A clichéd comment if ever she'd made one.

"A downside of the computer age," he said absently. Then he straightened up in his seat and sent her a sharp glance. "Listen, I've already been informed today that I'm a nosy brother, so I'm going to go with the role. What's happening between you and Garrett?"

Startled, she dodged the question. "What has he told you?"

"Nothing. That's why I'm asking."

"We were…attracted. But we've decided we can't make it work." She managed a small shrug. "That's all."

"I'd say a lot more than attracted, at least on Garrett's part. But maybe not yours?"

If only it were so simple. "That's not the problem."

"So what is it?"

Rachel suddenly remembered that Ford was a lawyer. "He's a minister."

"And?"

"I can't support him that way. Can't be part of a church. And since that's such a big aspect of his life, we would only end up hurting each other if we…got together."

"Garrett seems to be hurting pretty badly as it is." They traveled in silence for several minutes. Then Ford said, "What you're really afraid of, in my opinion, is that he'll change your mind."

"That's doubtful. I have my reasons."

"Caroline shared your mother's story with me. I'm sorry—I can't imagine what a painful experience you've endured. But there's a world of difference between Garrett and the man who duped her."

"Yes, there is. But believing in miracles and depending on prayer to solve your problems leaves you vulnerable. I choose to rely on facts, and on rational judgment." She took a deep breath. "I rely on myself."

"You must be very strong. Most of us need other people in our lives."

"I—" Her hands fisted in her lap. "I have friends."

"Which is why you moved—alone—to a little town in the middle of Wyoming."

"Bisons Creek wanted a doctor."

"You wanted to feel safe."

Rachel frowned at him. "How is that relevant?"

"We're talking about trust, and you won't."

She resorted to sarcasm. "You have me all figured out."

"I'm afraid so. Being part of a community entails trust, so you reject community. Love demands trust, so you push Garrett away."

With reluctance, she realized there was some truth to what Ford was saying. After the campfire, she'd promised Garrett she would try to trust him. But she'd failed.

Struggling to keep her voice steady, she said, "And do you have a solution for this dilemma?"

Ford sighed. "The same one we all face. You have to accept the risk."

That word again. Taking risks seemed to be the theme of the day.

He steered onto the exit for Interstate 25 south, a big loop that jostled the kids into waking up. "How much longer?" Thomas asked from the rear seat. "I'm hungry."

"Twenty minutes," Ford replied. "Will you survive?"

"I doubt it."

Everyone seemed more or less alive when the van doors opened, however, though the three steer riders moved a little slowly. "Man, oh, man, I'm stiff," Marcos complained. Then he grinned. "But I made the whistle."

Rachel went to Garrett's truck to get her duffel. "A successful expedition," Dylan said, pulling the bag out for her. "Everybody's home safe and sound."

Garrett came around the front end. "Now, of course, they're going to want to ride steers every day. We've created a problem for ourselves." His gaze met Rachel's. "Did you have a pleasant drive?"

"Great." *Especially the part where your brother cross-examined me.* "I'm happy my services weren't really necessary. Congratulations on pulling off your minirodeo."

He pretended to wipe the sweat off his forehead. "I have a few more gray hairs after the experience, but the kids are worth it."

"They're lucky to have you." She wouldn't see him again, Rachel realized, except for medical issues, or if they happened to run into each other in town. Her chest suddenly felt hollow, and she couldn't quite get her breath.

She bent to pick up the bag. "I'll be on my way," she said, pretending to adjust her grip. "Have a nice evening." Walking toward her car, she wondered if he'd come after her, as he often had, to open her door or tease her with some question she didn't want to answer.

But she reached the SUV alone. She unlocked the doors and stowed the medical bag without his help. Once inside, she let herself glance over to where they'd been standing. Garrett wasn't there.

Instead, she found him with the kids on the porch of the house, a grin on his face as he watched Thomas re-enact one of his rides.

He would be fine, she decided, as her SUV rumbled down the gravel drive. Between the ranch and the church and the kids, his life couldn't accommodate more commitments. A complicated relationship, as theirs must surely be, simply wouldn't fit.

Rachel decided she would be fine, too…as soon as she forgot the warmth of his smile, the strength in his hands, the taste of his mouth. His care and concern for others, his good-natured humor and his sense of responsibility—once she'd put those out of her mind, she'd be back to normal. Back to her rational, predictable, safe…

…excruciatingly lonely…new life.

Chapter Twelve

Garrett parked himself on the porch Tuesday evening while the kids played flashlight tag in the dark.

"How was your day at the office?" Caroline sat down in the rocker next to his.

Not a question he wanted to answer. Honestly, at least. "Busy. Phone calls, sermon notes. The usual. How did the farrier visit go?"

"Really well. Each of the kids got a chance to make noise on the anvil and they all took a shot at trying to hammer in a nail. Jo went into a lot of detail about the importance of hoof care, and she held their interest pretty well. This afternoon we worked on riding bareback in the corral. Everybody stayed on at the walk. But we now have seven pairs of jeans in the wash."

He managed a brief smile. "To be expected." Her concerned gaze predicted more uncomfortable questions. Garrett searched for a diversion. "Actually, I got three strange phone calls today. Three different people, all asking me to dinner."

"On the same night?"

"Different nights of this week. Wednesday, Friday and Saturday. And that's after lunch with the Bolans on Sunday. In five years, I've never had so many invitations so close together."

"It's not your birthday."

"Nope. And I just visited with them all at the party last Friday." A mental wince greeted the memory. There didn't seem to be anything he could call to mind that didn't evoke an image of Rachel. Eventually, he supposed, he would get used to the pain.

Caroline didn't say anything for a few minutes as the laughter and screams of the teenagers chasing each other filled the silence.

Then she put her hand on his arm. "I have to let you know—Ford talked with Rachel yesterday on the way home. About you."

"Well, damn him. He had no business butting in."

"He's concerned. We all are. I had dozed off, but I woke up to hear some of what they said… I'm sorry, Garrett."

"So much for suffering in silence." He put his hand over hers. "Thanks, Caroline. The odds were against me going in. I knew that."

"I wish I could do something…"

"Don't bother Rachel about this, please. If Ford questioned her, she's been badgered enough."

"Of course." She got to her feet. "So you'll be away tomorrow night, plus Friday and Saturday?"

"Sorry. I said yes to the first call, and then couldn't refuse the other two."

"We'll exact our revenge. The kids didn't get around to writing the thank-you notes for Dave. You can have the pleasure of encouraging them to do it after breakfast tomorrow."

His smile turned wry. "An even trade."

In fact, monitoring the teenagers as they cooked three meals was probably easier than convincing them to write neat, articulate letters. Lizzie and Nate listened to the guidelines and settled to the task, but the rest of the kids, even Becky, balked. Those with the most to be grateful for—the steer riders—complained loudest and longest.

"I understand you don't enjoy writing," he told them. "I don't care. This is the right thing to do and you will make the effort. Or else instead of going fishing, you'll spend this afternoon cleaning up the barn. I noticed lots of cobwebs in there this morning."

That threat earned the objectors dirty glances from the four kids who were working on their letters. Still grumbling, Marcos, Thomas and Lena bent over their papers. Most of the morning had passed before Garrett collected a readable, tidy note from each of them. Operating on yet another restless night, he was as drained by the process as if he'd written all seven messages himself.

At the creek that afternoon, Lizzie still refused to fish, but otherwise the trip kept everyone entertained.

Garrett appreciated having something to do; otherwise he tended to get lost in his thoughts—a desolate place to be lately. His life would continue to follow the path he'd chosen, enriched by his family, his congregation and their town, and, always, his absolute faith. Only two weeks ago, he'd have said he couldn't ask for more.

Then he'd met Rachel and fallen in love with her, and he'd discovered how much more he could want. How much more he could need. How the whole of his happiness could come to rest in the presence of one person...

"Hey." Dylan had come up beside him. "We have a problem. Watch Lena."

Garrett focused on the girl, who was baiting her hook. Trying anyway. She dropped the bait, bent slowly to pick it up and staggered, putting out a hand to recover her balance. When she straightened, she stared at her hands in confusion, as if she wasn't sure what to do.

In seconds he was standing beside her, and he could see moisture on her golden skin. "Lena? What's wrong?"

"Not feeling good." She swayed, putting a hand on his arm to steady herself. "Dizzy."

Warning flares went off in his head. "Did you take your insulin at lunch?"

"I did." Her eyes closed as she frowned. "Maybe."

Test, was all he could think as fear vibrated in his head. *She has to test her blood.* "Where are your supplies?"

"In…the truck."

Justino joined them. "What's the matter? Is she okay?"

"She'll be fine." Dylan tried to redirect him. "You can keep fishing."

The boy shook off his hand. "I'm not leaving."

Garrett shook his head. "Follow us, then. We're going to the truck." Setting an arm around the girl's waist, he walked her to the vehicle. The backpack lay on the passenger-side floorboard. "Lena, we have to test your blood. Can you handle that?"

She leaned against Justino, who put his arm around her. "What did I do wrong?"

Her question pierced his heart. "Nothing, sweetheart. We're just going to check your blood sugar." *Equanimity*, he recalled, hearing Rachel's voice. *First take your own pulse.*

He pulled in a deep breath and prepared to manage this crisis.

The process, with Lena dazed and practically helpless, seemed to take a long time. Cleaning her hands, preparing the meter, pricking her finger… Garrett had to will his own hands to stop shaking. The five seconds waiting for results lasted forever.

"Fifty-three. You're hypoglycemic, Lena. You need

sugar." Delving into the bag again, he found a can of orange juice. "It's warm, but it's sweet."

She made a disgusted face at the first sip. "Yuck."

"Drink the whole thing."

Once she'd finished, he handed her one of the cookies they'd brought along for a snack. "This will taste better."

"Not after juice," she protested, but surrendered when he glared at her. "Okay, okay."

Checking his cell phone while she ate, he found that he had no service—he couldn't call Rachel for advice. He and Lena would have to handle this on their own.

They tested twice more as she sat in the truck, head back and eyes closed.

Justino hovered beside her, his face anxious. "Is she going to be all right?"

"Eighty-eight," Garrett said, reading the third test. "You're coming into the normal range. Are you feeling better?"

"Not so dizzy. Or hot." She rolled her head from side to side on the seat. "Why did this happen to me?"

"Maybe you took too much insulin at lunch. Or didn't eat enough. Or for no reason at all that you can figure out."

Opening her eyes, she gave him a serious look. "I mean the diabetes. Why? Is God punishing me?"

"Absolutely not. God doesn't single out people to punish or to bless." Wishing Rachel were there, he called upon the medical information he'd absorbed. "Researchers believe diabetes is a genetic problem—you're born with the...the tendency. And then it's triggered by something—a virus, maybe, a minor illness you might not even have noticed, that messes up your pancreas. At least, that's what I've understood. But you haven't done anything to deserve diabetes. It's just what is."

"Lucky me." Lena sighed. "Can I go back to fishing? I think I'm okay."

He checked his watch. "It's late. We should head home. Why don't you sit and recover while I get the rest rounded up?"

By the time they reached the barn, Lena seemed almost normal. A little tired, maybe, but more or less herself.

"Take it easy tonight," Garrett advised. "Be sure you test before dinner and double-check the dosage. Your system has to regain its balance."

She rolled her eyes, indicating she'd at least recovered her attitude. "I know that." Then she smiled at him. "I should write you a thank-you note, too."

"Not necessary." But he went into the house to change for dinner with less of a cloud hanging over his head. His first instinct was to call Rachel and fill her in on what had happened—the emergency he'd dreaded had arrived and he'd coped successfully, with calm if not actual equanimity. He valued the boost to his confidence.

But he didn't make the call. That kind of sharing would only deepen a connection she didn't want. He wouldn't burden her further. After checking in with Caroline and reporting on Lena's situation, he headed into town, wondering during the drive why so many people suddenly wanted his company for a meal.

The answer waited for him at his destination, a nice two-story house not far from the church, where a green SUV with Washington state plates was parked on the shoulder of the road.

Rachel had been invited, too.

Taking into consideration the arch glances he'd received on Sunday from Martha Bolan, he didn't require help to figure out what the members of his congregation had planned. They'd observed their pastor with the new doctor at the party and decided to do a little match-making.

Garrett banged his forehead on the steering wheel. His instinct for self-preservation urged him to bolt, to get as far away as fast as possible. He could make his apologies over the telephone—a sudden violent stomach bug or a bad case of poison ivy. A rattlesnake bite. Anything to avoid the confrontation ahead of him.

The front door of the house opened. His host, Luis Alvarez, stepped out on the stoop and stood with his hands on his hips, staring at Garrett in the truck. Then Luis motioned for him to come in.

Trapped.

As reluctant as a condemned man on the way to his execution, Garrett crossed the grass and climbed the front steps.

"Good evening, Luis," he said, shaking the man's hand. "Thanks so much for having me over."

"Our pleasure, Pastor. Come on in." Leading the way through the house, Luis kept talking. "The weather's been so nice, we hated to waste the evening inside, so we decided to light the grill and enjoy dinner on the deck. Here we are." He opened a French door. "I'm going to bring the steaks. You just step on outside."

"Sure." Garrett squeezed his eyes shut for a second. Then, since he didn't have a choice, he crossed the threshold.

Alma, Luis's wife, jumped up from the table to give him a hug. "Welcome to our home." She stepped away, smiling. "And, of course, you know our other guest. We thought it would be fun if the four of us enjoyed dinner together."

"Definitely." He met Rachel's bright blue gaze with his own. "Glad you could come, Rachel."

"You, too." She appeared as uncomfortable as he would expect.

She also seemed to him to be the embodiment of summer, bathed in the golden glow of the afternoon sun, wearing a sleeveless yellow dress that skimmed her curves and left a nice stretch of slender legs bare, along with white sandals that showed off her pretty feet. Her toenails were polished bright orange.

Not a sight he would forget, for a long time to come.

"DID YOU *PLAN* THIS?" Rachel asked him when Alma went inside to get drinks.

"I wouldn't do that," Garrett said, bristling. "You really don't trust me, do you?"

"It's not that. I just… What would put this idea into their heads? They clearly believe we're a couple."

"I have my suspicions. Have you received other invitations? For this week?"

"Friday and Saturday." She stared at him in horror. "You, too?"

"We're the target of a plot." He pivoted as Alma stepped out carrying a tray of glasses. "Let me help you with that."

Luis appeared with a platter of steaks and the conversation centered on their family—they had a son in the army and a daughter living in California. Garrett seemed completely at ease—these were his church members, after all, and he'd served as their pastor for years. His genuine interest and enthusiasm for the details of their lives demonstrated why he was so well liked…so *loved*… by his congregation.

But if she and Garrett tried to have a relationship, not

sharing this important part of his life would only create a chasm between them. It was also possible her rebuff of the church would create problems for him. And when they broke up—as they surely would—the church members would lay the blame squarely on Rachel's shoulders. What kind of negative effect would that have on her medical practice?

"Do you have family, Rachel?" Alma asked as they ate. "I understand you grew up near Laramie?"

"I did, but my mother passed away a couple of years ago." She took a sip of water. "There's no one else."

"Oh, you poor thing." The older woman put a hand on Rachel's arm. "I'm so sorry. We'll adopt you. You can be part of our family." She sent a mischievous glance across the table. "Of course, Garrett has three brothers. I'm sure they've taken you in already."

"The Marshalls have been very kind." Rachel searched in desperation for a change of subject. "I taught a first-aid course for their camp kids last week. What's going on at the ranch has made a big difference in those young lives."

"I'm sure you two will work well together." Luis nodded at Garrett, and then at Rachel. "Bisons Creek is lucky to have you both."

"We're not—" Rachel started, then stopped when Garrett gave her a warning glance.

Alma stood up from her chair. "I'll clear these dishes so we can have dessert. I made your favorite, Pastor—chocolate fudge cake with chocolate ice cream. And chocolate sauce."

"Can we help?" Garrett asked. "The sooner to arrive at the cake?"

Laughing, Luis got to his feet. "You two just sit here and enjoy each other's company. We'll be right back."

Once the Alvarezes left, Rachel glared at Garrett. "Why did you stop me? We should clarify the situation."

The smile he'd been wearing since he arrived disappeared. "Why?"

"Because it's uncomfortable, having them assume that we're...that we're a couple. Embarrassing." And painful. But she kept that part to herself.

"If you tell them, *they'll* be uncomfortable and embarrassed. A nice evening will be spoiled. They mean well, so let's just leave them with their illusion. Eventually..." He took a deep breath. "Eventually they'll figure out the truth."

He was tired, she realized. Without someone to perform for, all the energy of his personality had waned.

Garrett was suffering as much as she was.

"Here we are." Alma emerged from the house with the cake and set it down in front of him. "For you."

In a moment, he recovered the facade. "Wow! It must be six layers high."

"Eight."

"Incredible. I can't wait to take a taste."

"I'll give you the recipe," Alma told Rachel. "It's much easier than it appears."

She summoned some energy of her own. "I can't wait to try it out."

At the end of the evening, she stood with Garrett outside the Alvarezes' front door to say good-night.

"You two shouldn't wait too long to seal the deal," Luis said them, shaking Garrett's hand. "You're not getting any younger."

"Autumn is a lovely season for a wedding." Alma folded Rachel into a hug. "We were married in October and couldn't have asked for a more perfect day."

Once they reached the street, Rachel found her voice.

"I suggest a notice on the bulletin board at Kate's Diner. Simple, succinct. 'Dr. Vale and Pastor Marshall are just friends.'"

"Just *casual* friends," Garrett added.

"Right." She reached her car and leaned against the fender, closing her eyes. "I'm exhausted." Garrett's truck was parked behind hers. So at least he'd been prepared, when he came in tonight, to see her.

"And we have another two dinners to endure." His gaze was bleak. "With more, I'd bet, in the planning stages."

Another risk occurred to her. "If they learn the truth after the fact, they may think we deliberately deceived them."

"A definite possibility." He rubbed his hands over his face. "Anyway, it would be rude to try and get out of Friday or Saturday night. Maybe Dylan can spread the word on Sunday that we broke up. A mutual decision."

"I suppose it's the best we can do." She attempted a smile. "At least they care about you."

Garrett blew out a short breath. "Sometimes people care too much." Turning on his heel, he went to the door of the truck, but then hesitated and retraced his steps. "I wanted to let you know—Lena had a low blood-sugar episode this afternoon. While we were fishing. Dizziness, confusion, clammy skin. I couldn't get a call to go through."

"Is she okay?"

"She'd brought her supplies, so I tested her and got some juice and a cookie into her. She recovered pretty fast."

"What was her reading?" Hearing the number, she blew a silent whistle. "Now that she's experienced the sensation, let's hope she won't wait as long to deal with it."

"Anyway, I thought you should know." He walked away again.

"Garrett?"

Though he stopped, he didn't face her.

"You dealt well with a real emergency." And not with prayer, but with cold, hard science. And no support. Lena was lucky to have him around. "Congratulations."

After a moment, he said, "Thanks." Then he climbed into his truck. At a loss, Rachel did the same, and they went their separate ways in the dark.

They met again Friday night at the Johnsons' for Italian food, and on Saturday at the Wilkeses', where they ate Tex-Mex with several other couples and played charades—a game at which Garrett proved to be a master. Rachel found his clues easy to read and their team won the match. The prize was his-and-hers argyle sweaters. Fortunately, the night was too warm to put them on.

Throughout the hours they spent together, Garrett met everyone's expectations—he joked and laughed, listened and spoke, in the same lighthearted way they were used to. If his face was drawn, no one said anything. They didn't notice that he played with his food but didn't really eat. They didn't see him at the end of the evening when he dropped the pretense and his strong, square shoulders slouched.

Rachel followed his example, doing her best to hide the despair. She responded to his wisecracks with her own grins, joining in on conversations with him as if nothing was wrong. They sat next to each other at tables and on the sofa, stood together by the pool. Their hands touched, occasionally, when passing dishes of food. Those were difficult moments.

More than once, she forgot they were pretending. When they were trading quips, when their gazes met and held, when they laughed together at someone's comment…the rightness of their connection often overwhelmed her common sense.

She always remembered their true situation, though, and landed back in reality with a thud. Garrett and she were not a couple, and wouldn't become one. His job and hers would be hampered, their relationships with the people in town threatened. Far safer not to try.

The phone rang on Sunday afternoon when she was trying—and failing—to focus on one of her favorite Louis L'Amour stories.

"Rachel, it's Alma Alvarez. You poor thing—I just heard."

For a minute, Rachel didn't understand. "I'm sorry. Heard what?"

"About you and Pastor Garrett. You must be devastated."

Dylan had obviously spread the news. "It's been difficult." That much was surely true.

"The way you two gazed at each other when you were at my house the other night, I would never have believed things weren't perfect between you. The expression in his eyes…"

Not something she wanted to hear. "We're planning to stay friends. Casual friends."

Alma gave a short laugh. "I've never seen that work out. Once you've been passionate about a man, you never truly forget. But don't worry," she said in a more cheerful voice. "We've adopted you and you'll stay part of the family. We'll just be sure not to invite you and Garrett to the same events, that's all. Maybe we can find you a handsome cowboy instead!"

At the end of the call, Rachel sat and stared at her phone. Alma hadn't reacted to the "breakup" as expected.

She hadn't blamed Rachel. Or Garrett, for that matter. And she'd seemed just as interested in a friendship with Rachel as she had before.

She was just one person, of course. Others—Ms. Simpson, for instance—might respond differently. But then again…maybe the repercussions Rachel had anticipated wouldn't occur.

Maybe their situation wasn't as dire as she'd believed. Had this just been another example of her failure to trust?

GARRETT FACED MONDAY morning with a distinct lack of enthusiasm. He'd fielded phone calls from church members until ten o'clock last night, all of them wanting to express their condolences over his breakup with Rachel—and probably to glean some details they could pass on. Upon finally falling into bed, he'd actually slept, but now was still tired. If he could have stayed under the covers all day, hiding from the world, he'd have done so.

Instead, he woke the boys and got them started on breakfast. He spent the morning in the corral, working with the kids on their bareback skills—Lizzie, in particular, was nervous about trotting without a saddle. After lunch, while Caroline and Ford supervised a hike in the foothills, he drove into town. Hayley Brewster had requested he visit.

He expected to find her tending the garden, her usual occupation during good weather, but her broad-brimmed straw hat and bright yellow gloves lay on a rocking chair on the porch. Behind its screen, the oak front door stood closed—another unusual sign. Wondering about the reason Hayley had wanted to talk with him, Garrett knocked on the door frame.

The wait seemed long, but at last the door opened.

Hayley stood in the shadowed entry hall. "Hello, Pastor. Come on in."

"No weeds to pull?" he asked, stepping inside. "You demolished them all?"

"No weeding today. Why don't we sit down?" She led the way to the living room on the right side of the door. Instead of her normal brisk stride, her walk seemed slow and stiff, as if she'd hurt herself.

"Everything all right?" Still standing, he watched as she dropped into a cushioned recliner rather than her usual choice of a ladder-back chair. "How are you feeling?"

She waved away his question. "I didn't ask you over to talk about me. Tell me the meaning of this nonsense between you and Dr. Vale."

"Nonsense?" Watching her, he realized she was quite pale under her tan.

"First I hear you're involved. Then you're not." Which—" Hayley gasped, and put a hand on her breastbone. "Which is it?" But her voice had weakened.

To hell with being interrogated. "Not. What's wrong?" Bending over her, Garrett noticed moisture on her forehead, and her hair was damp above her ears. "Tell me what's going on, Hayley."

She gasped again. "I've...been having...these pains." Her hand patted her chest. "They go away. Except today... they won't." Her attempt at a smile failed. "I'll be fine."

"God." It was a prayer. "You need to see Rachel. Now."

Hayley refused to be carried, so he kept his arm around her as she shuffled to his truck and climbed in. Behind the wheel, he took a couple of deep breaths, reaching for the equanimity Rachel had talked about. "Two minutes. We'll be there in two minutes."

They burst into the clinic in less than that. Allie

stared at them through the reception window. "What's the matter?"

"Chest pain," Garrett said, as calmly as he could.

"I'm fine," Hayley said again. "Don't make a fuss."

Allie had already come around to the door. "This way." She motioned them into the first examining room. "Sit her on the table." With Hayley seated, Allie nodded toward the hallway. "Out." The door shut behind him.

As he stood there, Rachel stepped out of the other room. "Garrett?"

"Hayley Brewster is having chest pain."

"So Allie said. We'll take care of her." She put a hand on his arm. "Try to relax." Then she knocked on the door and went into Hayley's room.

A minute later, Allie rushed out and down the hall, leaving the door open. Rachel stood beside the exam table, performing chest compressions on Hayley's motionless body.

Without pausing, she glanced at him. "Call 911. She's had a heart attack."

Chapter Thirteen

Allie hurried into the exam room with the defibrillator.

"Get the patches on." Rachel continued with chest compressions while the nurse charged the machine. "Ready?" Lifting her hands, she said, "Now."

Hayley jerked and then gasped. "Oh, my God!" She glared at Rachel. "What was that?"

Rachel pulled the edges of the patient gown together over Hayley's chest. "Your heart stopped. We gave you a shock to start it up again. I'm sorry—I know it hurts."

"Like being kicked by a mule."

Garrett came to the door. "The ambulance is on its way. Was that Hayley's voice I heard?"

"Pastor." Hayley stretched out an arm. "I'm in trouble here."

He stepped in and held her hand. "Dr. Vale's taking care of you. Just try to relax and let her work."

Grateful for his comforting presence, Rachel proceeded with the measures necessary to stabilize Hayley for the ride to the hospital. She checked the EKG frequently and was relieved that another defibrillation wasn't required.

The noisy arrival of the EMTs in the front of the office startled them all. Rachel briefed them on the situation and what she'd done, handing over the EKG strip. With admirable efficiency, the two men took over, bringing in a stretcher and preparing their patient for transport. "We'll carry her to Casper," the driver told Rachel. "It's the closest hospital for cardiac care."

But Hayley protested leaving. "I don't want to be alone. Pastor Garrett, please come with me."

He bent over her, clasping her hand. "You won't be alone." His voice was low and soothing, his gaze, holding hers, steady and confident. "God goes with you, watching over you every moment. And you have the hearts of all your friends. Just close your eyes and remember those who love you."

The fear eased out of Hayley's face. Eyes closed, she nodded. "You're right. I'll be okay." She folded her hands together at her waist as the stretcher rolled out the door. Garrett followed.

Rachel stripped off her gloves. "Good job," she told Allie. "We'll now return to our regularly scheduled program."

But when the nurse left the room, Rachel took a moment to sit down. She'd had an instant of alarm when she recognized the patient. Hayley was a beloved figure in Bisons Creek and in Garrett's church. With him standing there watching, Rachel had experienced an intense pressure to save this life.

Then her training had kicked in and she'd done her job, aware of whom she was working on yet able to remain objective. In the process, she'd begun to accomplish the purpose that had brought her to Bisons Creek—making a difference in the well-being of the community. The community of which she was gradually becoming a part.

And that surprised her. The townspeople hadn't waited for her to save a life before taking her into their homes, their hearts. Most didn't even seem to care whether she went to church or not. She had arrived with good intentions and they'd simply made her welcome.

Would it be that simple with Garrett? Could they possibly work this out?

In her preoccupation, she jumped when Allie came to the door. "Ms. Simpson is still waiting in exam room two."

"Right." She hurried down the hall, expecting a tongue-lashing. "I'm so sorry," she said as she opened the door. "The emergency was a matter of life and death, I'm afraid." Shoulders squared, she faced Ms. Simpson, prepared for the worst.

But Dorothy's expression was somber, and she seemed pale. "I opened the door," she said in a subdued tone, "to hear what was happening. Hayley Brewster had a heart attack?"

"I can't share medical information," Rachel said, as kindly as she could manage.

"Is she all right?"

"They'll learn more about her condition when she gets to the hospital." In sympathy, she added, "Garrett Marshall is with her."

"I have to go." Dorothy got to her feet. "I have to be there for her."

"But we haven't gone over your results—"

"Another day." Without ceremony, she brushed by Rachel and left the room.

With patients scheduled for the remainder of the afternoon, there wasn't a chance to follow up on Dorothy Simpson's reaction. Once they'd closed the clinic and locked the front door, however, Rachel asked Allie to satisfy her curiosity.

"Are Dorothy Simpson and Hayley Brewster close friends?"

"Since they were in school together. Seems strange, doesn't it? Mrs. Brewster is so nice and Ms. Simpson... isn't. They're both gardeners, and I guess that's what draws them together. That and their faith. The two of them are dedicated to the church."

Rachel recalled the way Garrett had eased Hayley's panic over being alone. His presence and his reassurance had made a significant difference in the older woman's outlook. Such confidence could only be a positive influence on her condition.

As she hadn't done in years, Rachel found herself envying that circle of trust.

At the hospital in Casper, she found Garrett and Dorothy Simpson in the waiting room.

"Blocked arteries," Garrett reported as she joined them. "Which the doctors say they've opened. She should be home in a few days." His relieved smile didn't conceal the traces of stress and worry on his face.

"We haven't been able to visit her." Dorothy sat holding her purse tightly in her lap. "She must feel so alone."

Rachel sat down beside her. "She's been pretty busy being treated," she said gently. "And she's had lots of nurses and doctors around her. I'm sure they'll let you in when she's settled."

Dorothy nodded but didn't seem convinced. Her stern gray gaze met Rachel's. "Thank you for your expertise, Dr. Vale. You saved Hayley's life today."

Seated on her other side, Garrett put a hand on Rachel's arm. "I haven't had a chance—"

"How is she?" Jim Bolan stopped in front of them, with Martha right behind him. "What do you know?"

Garrett stood to shake Jim's hand and relay the news.

Martha took his place beside Rachel. "I just can't believe this happened. Mrs. Brewster always seemed so well. It would be just terrible if we had lost her." She took Rachel's hand in both of hers. "Thank God she could get to your office for help. It's a miracle that you are here for us in Bisons Creek. Just a miracle."

Rachel wanted to set the record straight. "Garrett was actually visiting Hayley. He was the one who brought her to me. He's the hero in this situation."

"Well, of course." Martha hopped up to give Garrett a hug. "You're so wonderful. We all would be lost without you."

Flushing, Garrett patted her shoulder. "I wouldn't want to be anywhere else."

A nurse appeared at the doorway. "Mrs. Brewster can have visitors," he said into the sudden silence. "Two at a time for five minutes."

Dorothy got to her feet and, without a word to anyone, followed the nurse.

Luis and Alma Alvarez arrived while she was gone, along with another couple Rachel didn't recognize. She was introduced to the Fergusons as "our Bison Creek miracle worker" and barely refrained from cringing.

Then Dorothy tapped her on the shoulder. "Hayley wants to talk to you and Pastor Garrett."

As they went down the hallway, Garrett said. "You really were terrific this afternoon. I'm so grateful—"

Rachel held up a hand. "If you use the word *miracle*, I'll slap you."

He feigned alarm. "I wouldn't dare."

But Hayley did. Holding hands with both of them, she looked from one to the other. "The two of you worked a miracle for me today. Thank God for you both." Her expression grew mischievous. "It's a sign that you're meant to be partners."

Garrett's chuckle sounded forced. "Maybe you're still under the influence of some of those drugs, Hayley. But

I'm glad you're so much better than you were earlier. Is there anything you want from home? I'd be glad to bring a bag."

"Dorothy will take care of that. She's a curmudgeon, but she means well." She squeezed his hand, then let go and waved him away. "Now I want to speak to the doctor. You inform everybody that I'm fine and I'll see them tomorrow. No more visitors tonight."

"Sleep well," he said and, with a nod at Rachel, left the room.

"I'll come again," Rachel said. "We don't have to talk more tonight."

"Yes, we do. I've been considering your situation these past weeks. Now I'm here on the edge of death and I'd better speak up in case I don't get another opportunity."

"That's not going to happen." Rachel pulled over a chair and sat down. "But I'm listening."

"I wasn't afraid to die," Hayley said, her voice more tremulous than usual. "I've had a terrific life, great friends, a wonderful husband. The one thing I regret— we didn't have kids. Just didn't happen, though we tried. And that's what I want to say to you."

She closed both her weathered hands over Rachel's. "You're an honorable person, and you probably won't make terrible mistakes. What you'll regret, at the end, are the things you didn't do. Chances you didn't take to feel and to be. People you didn't love because you were afraid."

Rachel gazed at her, speechless.

Hayley sat forward in the bed. "You can't let hard times and hard-hearted people dictate your perspective on life. In this world, you have to choose to trust, dare to be open to all the possibilities. This old woman can assure you, what you stand to gain is far more than what you risk."

As Hayley reclined against the pillow, a nurse stepped up beside the bed. "Mrs. Brewster should rest now."

Rachel stood up and slipped her hand free. "Yes, she should." Leaning over, she kissed the older woman's cheek. "Thank you," she murmured. "I will remember."

"I'm counting on it." The irrepressible reply came with a wink.

Garrett waited in the hallway. "You're smiling, so the talk can't have been too serious."

Rachel headed in the direction of the waiting room. "Some advice from 'the edge of death.'"

"And what was that?"

She quoted, "'You can't let hard times and hard-hearted people dictate your perspective on life.'"

"Ah. I never doubted that Hayley Brewster was a wise woman." He blew out a breath and rubbed a hand over the nape of his neck. "It's been a long day."

"You can go home and get some rest. Mrs. Brewster is in excellent hands."

"I'm still on duty."

They came to the door of the waiting room and Rachel noted that even more church members had arrived, so the gathering now resembled a cocktail party. "Do they expect to be able to visit her?"

"Not tonight. They're just celebrating Hayley's survival, her life in general. You could call it an informal service of thanksgiving." Taking a deep breath, he straightened his shoulders. "And I should be in there. I'll make your excuses."

His tired eyes met hers, and she wanted more than anything to ease the load on his shoulders, restore his resilient spirit.

"It's still early," she said, surprising herself. "I'll come in with you."

By Wednesday night, Hayley's room resembled her garden, filled with blooming flowers of every color and variety.

"You'll have to hire a van to get these home tomorrow," Garrett joked when he walked in. "Or maybe a tractor trailer."

"They're all beautiful, but I can't keep them. Some of the folks from church will be taking them to nursing homes." She frowned at him. "You're seeming awful weary, Pastor. You're not supposed to run yourself ragged coming here so often for me."

"You're not to blame. We're baling hay on the ranch this week, as well as keeping the kids occupied. We took them up to Lake DeSmet to go boating yesterday. It's a demanding job, making sure seven kids don't drown."

"And maybe you're not sleeping too well, fretting over a certain pretty doctor in our town?"

Garrett shrugged a shoulder. "It will get better. I hope."

A knock on the door heralded the arrival of the person under discussion. "What will get better? Is something wrong?" She'd obviously come from work; she still had her white coat on over a pretty green dress.

"Not a thing." Hayley held out her hand for Rachel to take. "But as I just told the pastor, you shouldn't wear yourself out driving down here."

She did seem drained, her face pale. "I have to keep track of my patient. Is she behaving herself?" she asked him with a teasing lift of her brows.

The conversation remained lively, but Rachel seemed preoccupied. Her laugh didn't come as easily; her smiles seemed forced. Judging by Hayley's narrowed eyes, she noticed the same thing.

The Johnsons arrived for a visit, and so he and Rachel

left together, which gave him a chance to investigate. "Everything all right?"

After a moment, she said, "Of course. I've just been… busy." With a shake of her head, she made a visible effort to brighten up. "Is there a crowd in the waiting room again tonight?"

There was, and she joined him as she had Monday and Tuesday, listening to and empathizing with folks as they shared their worry and relief. He heard the *M* word frequently—miracle—and suspected how the idea must grate on Rachel. But she never betrayed her personal doubts.

The visitors left in twos and threes until, at last, they were alone.

"And then there were none," Garrett commented. "I don't know about you, but I'm talked out."

Rachel didn't answer. Standing by the window, she stared through the blinds into the night, her arms hugging her waist.

He stayed where he was, giving her space. "Are you okay?"

She didn't move. "Not really."

"What happened?"

"Nothing. All the gratitude, though…it gets to be too much."

"Salt in the wound?" he guessed.

Her brows lowered in a frown. "There's no wound."

"Oh, Rachel, of course there is. You're deeply injured. That's why you're angry." It was past time to confront her demons.

"Well…" She drew a deep breath. "Yes. I'm angry at the man who cheated my mother."

"That's a start. Did you ever get to tell him so?"

"I was never able to speak to him."

"You should have been able to yell at him, confront him with what he did."

She met his gaze, a reluctant smile curving her mouth. "That would have been great."

"You still could. Whether he hears you or not."

"Is this a therapy session? You said you were talked out."

Garrett shrugged. "Whatever works. Who else are you angry with?"

She faced the window again. "No one that I can think of."

"Come on. You don't have any reaction to the fact that your mother wouldn't follow your advice as a doctor? That she chose to believe a charlatan rather than her own child?"

"Hurt, perhaps… I don't want to be angry with a dead person."

"Doesn't matter what you *want*. You're a doctor. You're familiar with the five stages of grief. Anger is one of them. While you're yelling at the con man, you can yell at your mom."

Rachel didn't smile at that idea.

He kept pushing. "What about your responsibility for her death?"

"I did everything possible!" She glared at him. "Made appointments, brought home information, talked and talked and talked…" When he started to say something, she cut him off with a chop of her hand. "And I couldn't save her—couldn't do anything to make a difference." She strode across the room to stand right in front of him. "Hell, yes, I'm angry. At her for resisting, at myself for failing. At a world as broken, as wretched as this one." Putting up her hands, she wiped tears off her cheeks.

Garrett took those hands, led her to a chair and sat down beside her, waiting.

For long moments, she stared at her fingers, twined in her lap.

"What's on your mind?" he asked, finally.

"I didn't realize…how angry I was." Rachel glanced up at him. "But you did."

"And because you were angry, you isolated yourself from people who could comfort you. People who would care about you. You've been strong. But everybody needs help now and then."

"Isn't that a bit like the pot calling the kettle black?"

He had to admit, he had taken on way too much in the past several weeks. But the crises with Lena and with Hayley had shown him that he couldn't fix everything. Occasionally, he had to step away and let things happen as they would. He'd been attempting to do the same with Rachel. He just had to have a little more faith that things would work out.

"Equanimity, yes, I remember," he said. "I'm trying."

She almost smiled. "I don't know what to do now. I'm…adrift."

"Forgiveness is always a great start."

Her startled gaze met his. "You want me to forgive the man who—"

"No. Well, not to begin with, at least. Forgive yourself, Rachel. And forgive your mom. What happened can't be changed. Accept that and move on."

A long sigh escaped as her shoulders slumped. "Bad things still happen."

"But so do the good things. You came to Bisons Creek and Hayley Brewster is alive today because of that. Lena Smith is successfully managing her health issues because you're here. We can't explain why tragedies occur in this life. All we can do is love our neighbors and ease suffering where we find it. You're already an expert in that endeavor."

"And you're an extraordinary man, Garrett Marshall." She put a hand on his knee. "When I told a friend of mine about you, she wanted me to lower my defenses, give you a chance. But she wouldn't explain why. Now, I understand."

"What do you understand?"

"I needed to hear what you had to say. I needed… connection." Standing, she held out her hand. "Come walk me to my car. It's time we both went home."

The rest of the week passed in a blur for Garrett. Ranch work, camp work, checking on Hayley, writing Sunday's sermon—every hour had its assigned task, but with never quite enough hours in the day to get them all finished.

At least he was sleeping better, due solely to the fact that Rachel called every night late in the evening, after the kids were in bed.

When he first heard her voice over the phone, he panicked. "What's wrong? Has something happened to Hayley?"

"No, no, everything is fine. I just wanted to…talk."

"Oh." His heart rate stayed fast. "Like casual friends?"

"Um…not casual."

He grinned to himself. "We can definitely do that."

On Saturday, they talked until after 1:00 a.m., which left Garrett seriously short of rest. He was still yawning as he readied the church for the morning service at eleven. As usual, however, when he put on his robe a sense of calm and purpose came over him, and he felt ready to fulfill his mission. After a brief prayer for guidance, he left his office and made his way to the sanctuary.

In the moments before the service began, he surveyed the congregation, taking an informal census. Hayley sat in her usual place, with Dorothy beside her and her friends in the surrounding pews. Wyatt and Susannah sat close to the front and Caroline would be in the choir loft behind him. Ford and Dylan had stayed home to keep an eye on the teenagers, who weren't required to attend church.

Just as the choir stood up behind him to begin the opening song, a woman slipped through the closed doors to the entry hall. She hesitated, searching for an empty spot, and finally settled on the far end of a pew about halfway along. Watching her, Garrett had some trouble getting his breath.

Rachel had come to church.

Somehow, he got through the hour smoothly enough and managed to deliver his sermon without stumbling. The subject was forgiveness, because that had been on his mind. He could only hope Rachel heard the concern and caring behind the words.

Then the bells started to ring as the service ended. He made his way to the front door and tried to focus on each person who came through to shake his hand, all the while wondering when *she* would arrive, what *she* would say.

She was the last person in line. "No lightning bolts," she said, shaking her head. "I'm truly amazed."

He held her hand in both of his. "God gives everyone a second chance. Welcome back."

"Thanks. It feels—" she turned her head and gazed into the sanctuary "—right."

"I didn't expect to see you here so soon." Out of the corner of his eye, he noticed members of the congregation on the sidewalk, observing this meeting.

But Rachel was smiling at him. "I decided that if I was dating a minister, I should probably show up at church."

His pulse rate jumped. "Dating?"

"Isn't that what you do, before you get engaged?"

"Usually." He swallowed hard. "Is that your plan?"

Both her hands now clasped his. "It's a risk I wouldn't take with anyone else in the world."

The words warmed him like sunshine after a savage storm. "I love you," he said. "And I'm going to kiss you."

Rachel laughed. "There are people watching."

"Let them watch." Garrett pulled her into his arms and found her mouth with his. A sense of welcome, of homecoming, swept through him as she yielded to his hold and linked her hands behind his neck. Soft, warm lips, the sweet taste of her and the pounding of her heart against his chest assured him that this woman was, indeed, the answer to his prayers.

Lifting his head, he stared into her beautiful blue eyes. "You're sure you don't believe in miracles?"

"I'm starting to," she said.

"Right answer," he told her. And kissed her again.

Ten Months Later

THE WALK FROM Hayley's house only took a few minutes. As they stepped onto the front porch of the house they now shared, Garrett released Rachel's hand and reached into his pants pocket. "I made sure to have my key, since I doubted you would."

"Good plan." She stood close to his side, and he caught a drift of the scent she wore, the one he'd given her for Christmas. "This dress didn't come with pockets."

"But it's beautiful." He finished with the lock and gave her a quick kiss. "You're a beautiful bride. And now…"

Pushing the door open, he took a step and then swept her up into his arms. "Welcome home, Mrs. Marshall."

She laughed as he stepped over the threshold. "You're crazy."

"You've said that before." With the door shut behind them, he bent his head to hers. "Crazy about you."

They'd kissed at the altar, a sweet declaration of commitment in front of a church full of friends. The beginning of their life together.

But this was different. After so many cautious months, he wasn't holding back. Finally, he could offer the woman he loved all of himself.

Rachel responded with an intensity that matched his own, her mouth seeking, giving, demanding as the passion ignited between them. Without breaking the kiss, Garrett shifted his hold, letting his arm slide up along her legs as she straightened out against him. The ruffled layers on her pretty white dress rucked up, allowing his hand to graze the bare skin of her thigh. He groaned deep in his throat as he bent to let her feet reach the floor.

"You feel incredible," he murmured against her lips. She smiled.

"I'm planning to feel even better."

Lifting his head, he grinned. "I like the way you think." A glance around the room showed him a platter of food from the reception and a cooler containing a bottle of champagne resting by the couch. "Someone was here before us."

She turned to see, still leaning against him. "That's sweet. I noticed Caroline and Ford disappeared for a little while."

He circled his arms around her waist. "How could you tell, with so many people? But it was a fun reception."

"Hayley was sweet to host it in her garden. Springtime in Wyoming is so beautiful—I love the contrast of the blooming flowers down here and the snow still on the mountains."

"And it was nice of the kids to get all dressed up and join us."

"Even Thomas and Marcos. Ms. Simpson said they've had a successful school year."

"She has a one-track mind." Right now, Garrett did, too. But he could still be patient. "Shall I pour you some champagne?"

"Later." Rachel faced him, and her hands came to his shoulders. "Right now, I want you out of this jacket." She pushed the sleeves down his arms, then threw the coat over a chair. "And you can lose the tie." Her fingers found the knot.

His breathing had speeded up. "It's a nice turquoise tie. Matches your boots."

The tie landed on the coffee table. His shirt buttons somehow came undone, the tail dragged out of his pants. Then she took his hand and led him down the hall.

A new bed filled the space, big enough for the two of them. His shirt dropped to the floor.

Standing behind her, he pulled down the zipper on the lacy white dress, feeling his heart start to pound at the exposure of creamy skin underneath. Rachel caught the dress as it fell and stepped away to drape it over the armchair.

Then she came to him, wearing silky white lingerie and those turquoise boots. Her blue eyes were shining. "Make love to me, Garrett. The time is finally right."

He took her in his arms. "My pleasure."

But time had ceased to matter. In the sunny silence of late afternoon, they came together without reserve or restraint. Desire and delight were their only guides when

Garrett and Rachel seized their moment, honoring each other as husband and wife.

Afterward, they lay tangled together, catching their breath. Garrett wanted to say something to mark the moment, something meaningful and profound. As satisfied and happy as he'd ever been, he was having trouble coming up with the words.

Rachel stirred against him and pressed her head into his shoulder. "I love you," she said, in a drowsy voice.

He smiled up at the ceiling. "I love you, too."

And, really, what else mattered?

Funny how a day could turn out to be absolutely perfect, without changing at all.

* * * * *

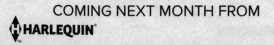

When a one-night stand with Violet Hathaway results in
an unexpected pregnancy, Cole Dempsey must put his
rodeo past behind him and embrace his new life as a
cattle rancher...or lose the woman he loves.

Read on for a sneak peak at
HAVING THE RANCHER'S BABY,
by Cathy McDavid from her
MUSTANG VALLEY miniseries!

"What are you doing here on your day off?" he asked.
"It's Sunday. The day of rest."

"Yeah, well, no rest for the wicked."

He let his voice drop and his eyes rove her face. "You're
not wicked, Vi." Though she could be flirtatious and fun
when she let loose.

For the briefest of seconds, she went still. Then—
strange for her, as Violet usually oozed confidence—she
turned away. "I asked you not to call me that."

"I like Vi. It suits you."

And it was personal. Something just the two of them
shared. Calling her Vi was his way of reminding her
about the night they'd spent together, which he supposed
explained her displeasure. She didn't like being reminded.

She'd made the mistake of telling him that Vi was a
childhood nickname, one she'd insisted on leaving behind
upon entering her teens. They'd been alone, lying in bed
and revealing their innermost feelings. Unfortunately, the
shared intimacy hadn't lasted, disappearing with the first
rays of morning sunlight.

"I was wondering. If you weren't busy later…" She let the sentence drop.

"I'm not busy." Cole leaned closer, suddenly eager. "What do you have in mind?"

Could she have had a change of heart? They weren't supposed to see each other again socially or bring up their one moment of weakness. According to Vi, it had been a mistake. A rash action resulting from two shots of tequila each, a crowded dance floor and both of them weary of constantly fighting their personal demons.

Cole didn't necessarily agree. Sure, the road was not without obstacles. As one of the ranch owners, he was her boss. On the other hand, *she* oversaw *his* work while he learned the ropes. Confusing and awkward and a reason not to date.

But incredible lovemaking and easy conversation didn't happen between just any two people. He and Vi had something special, and he'd have liked to see where it went, obstacles be damned.

Strange, he hadn't given her a second thought before their "mistake." One moment on a dance floor and, boom, everything had changed. A shame she didn't feel the same.

Unless she did and was better at hiding it? The possibility warranted consideration.

"We need to, um, talk." She closed her eyes and pressed a hand to her belly.

Don't miss
HAVING THE RANCHER'S BABY
by Cathy McDavid, available June 2016
wherever Harlequin® American Romance®
books and ebooks are sold.

www.Harlequin.com

Same great stories, new name!

In July 2016,
the HARLEQUIN®
AMERICAN ROMANCE® series
will become
the HARLEQUIN®
WESTERN ROMANCE series.

Connect with us to find your next great read, special offers and more.

f /HarlequinBooks

🐦 @HarlequinBooks

www.HarlequinBlog.com

www.Harlequin.com/Newsletters

 HARLEQUIN®

A *Romance* FOR EVERY MOOD™

www.Harlequin.com

HWR2016